Hawking Radiation

Ishmael A Soledad

ISBN: 1976374375
ISBN-13: 978-1976374371

For

Kitty for having not seen and yet believed

and

Andrew G McCann for prising the door open

CONTENTS

ACKNOWLEDGMENTS

Cover image courtesy NASA

Quote in *Transition* from the Holy Bible : Revised Standard Version courtesy W.M. Collins Sons & Co. Ltd.

THE LEAVING

So that was it. Plain. Simple. Easy as you like. Standing in the hallway bag clasped in each hand, wearing the jeans and boots I'd bought for her twenty-fifth, smile on her face.

"I'm going. Goodbye."

"That's it?" Five years together and she's there like Mary Poppins, looking past me out the front door. At least she has a single tear.

"Who is it?"

"Who's who?"

"Dave from the gym? Peter?"

"None of the above Phil, you know it's only you."

"Not" oh God no "Jenni from work?"

"Get real – I've said it once. It's no-one else."

She's out on the doorstep. A moonless night, the stars gaze down coldly on our fifty acres, our place. Wonder if she'll buy it out from me or force the sale?

"Where will you be? Will I see you again?"

"Dunno." she mumbles, looking at her watch. "Should be here soon."

"At least tell me why. I mean, you only said you'd leave this place for one thing. I have to at least know what I've done."

At this she turns to face me, finally look me in the eyes. I see she really isn't smiling. It's a grimace, fear and longing rolled into one. Uncertain, yet determined. Her makeup is tracked, more than one tear it seems.

"I did ask" she says slowly "but they said no."

"What?"

"Well," and by now she was slowly dissolving into a multi colored shaft of light "they only asked me."

GIANT

The taxi disgorged the five of us and, after pressing a few bills into the driver's hands, we walked quickly through the archway into the maze of alleys and streets inside the old city. Technically the whole area was off limits but no-one really enforced that rule for the last one earthside. Chances were for a lot of the guys it was the last one, period. Most usually went the whole hog, not infrequently being poured back to base from inside a rust lined cell courtesy of the city's finest, and it seemed that everyone took the whole ritual in stride, a thing to be humored, tolerated.

This was our last time, a few hours of freedom, and I knew that the other four were going to make the most of it. The old man of the group at thirty one I was also ten centimeters shorter and ten to fifteen wider across the shoulders which, at times, has not been too slight a disadvantage. The oldest of them was twenty two, in the camp the nearest to me being twenty five, so perhaps it was unusual I'd been adopted by these four. Or maybe not.

Tonight I was their chaperone, their guardian angel, keeping their money, my head and sobriety while they continued on their way. I looked out of place with my four companions as we strode down the boulevard, lolitas and sirens calling from open doorways, tousled locks and bouncing tattoos. They stood out in scarlet trimmed indigo blue uniforms, caps lofted at a rakish angle, boots mirroring the street lights. I blended into the background in my civvies and scuffed shoes, virtually hidden in their midst. Coming to the central plaza we stopped and I handed them their first tranche of the night's money, enough for their first two hours, and we split up noting to meet again at the plaza. Although hungry they preferred their first meal to be taken horizontally which for me was not an option, so I headed for a small brasserie across the way for some proper nourishment.

First impressions are seldom wrong, and I felt at home once I walked in the door and nearly choked on the acrid cigarette smoke hanging below the ceiling. Finding an unoccupied stool against the far end of the bar I laid my money down and signaled for a beer, the barmaid wallowing over and placing a nearly clean glass in front of me. I pushed a bill towards her. She went to pick it up but saw my signet ring.

"Going or back?"

"Going. Four a.m. tomorrow."

She smiled, front teeth tarred and stained, and pushed my money back to me with a huge paw. "Won't need that. Lost them" with which she jerked a thumb at a framed photo of two fresh faced kids hanging on the back wall "two years ago today on Five. Just remember."

I raised my glass in the picture's direction. "Jets."

She wiped a small tear from her eye with a corner of her stained apron. "Yeah, Jets."

I wouldn't say I was depressed. I don't get the dumps, I've had too much shit in my life to worry like that, but I was in what I refer to as my 'Sunday afternoon in the rain before Monday at work' mood – a flatness that is neither here nor there. The brasserie and I were a type then, perfectly in step with each other.

A sirloin and a beer steadied my mood a little bit, and I pulled out my photo of Cyn and propped it up against the empty glass which, to my lessening surprise, was filled again within minutes. Married four years, first child two months away, this small furlough was not long enough to get me across to Shepparton no matter how I went about it.

When I had called to let her know I was off she was out at her painting class. I must have looked pathetic on the answering machine, even the house I'd programmed with the Danny DeVito optional personality appeared genuinely upset with the news. The cat also promised to be on its best behavior while I was away. I've never really trusted cats, and it was on our bed preening itself when it said so, so I'm not sure. Anyway, it's Cyn's problem now not mine.

The place was slowly starting to fill and I was wondering if I should move on when someone tapped me on the shoulder. I turned to see a shrunken old man leaning on a cane, pointing with his free hand to the stool next to me. "Excuse me, is this seat taken?"

I smiled. "No," generous as always with what's not mine "feel free. Can I buy you a drink?" especially as they were on the house.

"No, thank you," with which two beers appeared as if by magic in front of us "but I would like to offer you one."

I thanked him, noticing he wasn't so much as old as worn out. I put him at my age plus about ten or so years, but the stoop of his shoulders and thin, greying hair gave the impression of a person seventy or so years into life. His face was lined, not deeply but often, and his skin had the mottled look of someone who had spent too long under a sun lamp. His smile disclosed a missing tooth which, in this day and age, was either laziness or vanity. I had known people who had grown up on the streets of Sao Paulo and Tokyo and survived; they looked used, this guy simply looked as if he hadn't made it out alive.

He took a lazy sip from his glass and placed it neatly down on the coaster, hands steady. Leaning back he studied me out of the corner of his eye, looking first at my hand clasping the bar and then to my face.

"Not one to wear your uniform I see. You must pardon my curiosity but I'd guess that you're off shortly, probably your first too by your face."

"Don't care too much for impressing people with spit and

polish," I countered "I've found it easier to get along if I blend in." I turned to face him. "Besides, as you said I'm off soon and I'm wanting a little slice of normal before the whole thing starts. Anyway, how'd you know?"

"It's the signet ring, you still look a bit uncomfortable wearing it. After a while most end up feeling like it belongs." He spun his drink lazily, the condensation pooling and spreading, slowly seeping into the fibers of the coaster. He wore the same signet ring as I did, a small silver and pewter affair with the southern cross above a clenched fist embossed on its face. Mine was shiny and less than two weeks old; his had dulled to grey, with nicks and cuts across and around it. A small scorch mark on the band blended with scarring along his finger. Pulling the bowl closer he put a handful of nuts in his mouth and, between chews, asked me why I was going. Damned strange question I thought, in particular coming from him, and I told him so.

He just smiled. "You see, some do it 'cause they want the excitement, the rush, to really feel like it's all on the line all the time. Others, they've got things to run from, things they don't want to see or hear of again, and this is the quickest and best way they can leave. For some it's all they can do to earn a dollar, get a clean bed and two meals a day. And then there's conscripts. Just trying to figure out where you fit in, though it don't seem you do. You're not runnin', you've brought your past with you," pointing to Cyn's photo "and you sure aren't an ego freak. And you also seem intelligent enough to avoid the draft. So I'm just curious."

I couldn't get angry. He might be a nosey old bastard but I'd wanted company. I laughed. "Yeah, none of the above. I volunteered for the degree." Even though I had brains, university education was far too expensive for me to even think of. I could pass all the entrance tests, but as I was non-minority and not connected I would have to be full fee paying – basically an impossible situation. However by joining the forces, doing a two year off world tour and staying on the reserves at home the government would pay for all my education at any level once I got back. That was my only reason for joining, my only reason for staying, and I told him as much.

He quietened down after that for a time, draining his glass and getting a refill. I changed to orange juice and checked the time. He leant back further on the stool, back resting on the faux wood of the wall, and his eyes seemed to glaze over. Shoulders drooped, he started to speak in low, measured tones betraying weariness and melancholy. "Let me tell you a little story," he began, and I swear even to this day that the bar became deathly still, even the barlady's frenetic movements slowing down "of a time and place not so far away …"

"I landed on Five with a squad of thirty fresh out of the Academy, two days after we had established the beachhead. I don't know much of those two days before I got there, but the wreckage and desolation told me all I needed. Five's like Earth, and I suppose that's the root of the problem. It's green, oxygen in the air, and life everywhere except where we went. The neutron weapons had killed everything for two hundred clicks, and the fire fight had burnt every building, every tree, every blade of grass to a crisp. Where we bivouacked that night had been a city of fifteen millions, all I could see of it was a small concrete stump near the horizon. By day it was worse. Every step crunched on burnt things, maybe animal maybe vegetable, I don't know, and horizon to horizon was charred, blackened plains, our ships, our guys, our weapons, and hundreds of thousands of grey puffs where our feet trod. Our first duty was grave digging, or should I say open pit burial. We put five thousand of them into a hole that first day and another five thousand each day after, and we were only a small part of the guys doing that. Not that we minded any, these were the enemy and so what if there were a few children in there, they'd only just grow up and shoot you anyway so it's better they're dead sooner."

"A week into it and we learned that we were going to take Five the hard way, the old way, inch by inch and yard by yard, conventionally. Someone up there," with which he flailed his hand wildly at the ceiling "decided that we needed Five intact, and as we could kill their nukes before they could use them, why not? Ha! Why not indeed."

"So we fought. I don't know to this day exactly where, and I don't know exactly how long, but I know it was forever. My squad, I lost them all one by one, the best men and women I knew, some quick and some slow. Got to where it was just me and those two" pointing at the photo over the bar "left of the originals. Father, son and holy ghost they called us, the trinity, thought we were invincible, and every rookie that joined and every rookie that died thought the same way."

"I saw people killed in ways that just ain't right, poisoned food, poisoned air, things that came out the soil at night and cut your throat, animals that explode on sight, all kinds of things. Saw one grunt stoop to pick up and smell a daisy. She died five minutes later from a new strain of ebola they'd developed, lying screaming and crying as the blood poured out her skin. Took an hour to burn that field of flowers it did."

"And we killed too, like after like. I was there when we tried out the new cholera strain, two million dead in a week. I recall poisoning a city's water supply, burning homes and families, shooting at civilians running away, letting prisoners escape carrying implanted bombs they didn't know about, timed to detonate when they got home. All on orders, but the orders didn't matter, we would have done it all the same without orders. They were the enemy, they had to die, and we were going to do that as efficiently and as quickly as we could."

He looked me in the eye, cold and hard. "Ever killed a woman with your bare hands?" Sweating, I regretted changing from beer to orange juice some moments back, the lump in my throat hardening.

"When it's a man it's easy, it's just another guy, another idiot who'd kill you soon as look at you. But a woman. They look like us on Five you know, heard they're more human than some of our kids, and that makes it worse. We'd just taken a position when these three attack us hand to hand. My two took the others and I was left with the third who had me on my back with a knife at my throat before I knew what hit me. Even through the camo she was good looking, small with red hair and green eyes, my 'type' I suppose but screaming at me and toting the biggest knife I'd seen." He drained his glass in a swallow, a faint trembling in his hands.

"She fought hard, but in the end I had her, hands round her neck squeezing the life out of her. You know, I've done my share of men like that, some curse you as they die, some fight to the end, others just let go and accept. Some, a few, will cry and plead and it makes you hate them for not being men, for being cowards, for making you deny them mercy you can't give. But a woman. She cried as she went, looking at me with the question in her eyes and there's nothing I can do. She was young, could've been my sister or my lover, but she was the enemy." He looked down. "She was the only one I stopped to bury. Maybe that's where it started."

He stayed silent for a while, the bar with him.

"It was about two weeks maybe after that we got the news. We were to have the man himself, the four star General, Batlow, join us for a push into the enemy's central area. He had a reputation nearly as good as ours, always seemed to be in the thick of the fight, always taking big risks, always being the soldier's soldier. Every week his picture would be in the vids as he led from the front and dragged everyone after him. We knew casualty rates hit the roof wherever he went, but hell, might as well die in good company. 'Iron Arse' they called him, got it from catching a hollow point in the butt early on and having a plate put in as part of the reconstruction. He was a hero to most of the guys and an inspiration. Tough, dedicated, fearless, leading by example. Or so we thought."

"Which is why I couldn't make out my Captain's mood when he told me my squad would be working closest with Iron Arse. It was almost as if he felt he was a traitor, maybe selling us out. Me and the guys couldn't have been happier and me and the trinity the most, I mean, the guy was an absolute legend."

"When I finally saw him he was standing on the top of an

APC, a tower of pure muscle, sweat soaking through his fatigues and an attitude you could feel that'd kill at a hundred meters. His eyes were lit up like beacons, challenging us as he stabbed at a map tacked to the turret, 'The capital city boys' he yelled, 'were goin' all the way and take the fight to these bastards right in their own homes and show them what war's about.' and I was screaming and whooping along with the rest of them, couldn't wait to get out there and get going. 'And you know what' he called, jumping down and striding through the crowd to me 'I'm getting the best beside me.' and he threw his arms across me and the ghost's and son's shoulders, 'Me and the trinity's going in first and bringing hell with us!' and the roar nearly broke my ears, and I'm yellin' louder than ever and there's guns going off in the air and the whole bit. March into hell? Shit, would've gone back and lived there if he would've asked."

"Hyped couldn't come near what we felt, it was like I'd been pumped full of dust and wasn't coming down for a month, the rest of 'em felt the same, right up to the time we hit the dirt at our IP." He drew deeply from the glass, moving the foam from his lips with a worn and callused thumb.

"We pulled a small hill on the north side of the city, the top looked across the whole place, clear up to the mountains behind. Pure rock, boulders everywhere, the hill had saddles either side lain with mines and traps, leaving only one way to go – over the top – straight through the enemy's killing zone, right where he wanted us. So up we went, or at least we tried. Ten seconds after we dropped I'd lost six to snipers and two to booby traps. I was wearing someone's blood on one sleeve and had a particle beam burn across my leg by the time I'd flattened out, trying to burrow my way into the gravel scree and pull my arse down as low as my belly. I lay there looking round for a good couple of seconds and right then and there I knew I was going to die. The hill was only a hundred or so meters high and maybe five times as wide, with no cover or vegetation. All the way up was boulders and caves, you could've hidden an army in there and no-one would know, and that's exactly what they'd done. I could see dozens of winking lights and puffs of grey smoke coming from the hill, each one ending with a crunch or a cry from our lines. Nothing for it I thought, and I led the boys up into it."

He paused again, briefly, before continuing. "Still don't know to this day quite how we did it, but six hours later I was perched at the top of that hill, firing into the valley below. I'd started with thirty men under me, and thirty other squads with us, and when I got to the top it's just me, the trinity, and two others; the other squads weren't much better off. For all the weapons, technology, and gear we had, after the first ten minutes we'd fought hand to hand, belly down and crouching, for every meter of that rock. I used knives, rocks, anything I could get my hands on to batter my way through. It was medieval, bits of blood and body caking the earth and us, you couldn't see our fatigues or faces for clotted blood and dirt, burns and cuts. The holy ghost had lost his hair and helmet, both burned off early on, and the son had a gash the length of his left arm. But we were all still alive, still there."

"And then he arrives, old Iron Arse, with forty of the meanest son of a bitch marines I'd ever seen. Standing there in his spotless uniform, reflective sunnies and all, smiling at us. 'Great work men' he crowed, 'fantastic job' with which he strides to the crest of the hill and poses with the city to his back as the two photographers he brought with him went about their work. 'Don't forget my left side's the best side' he quipped, and with the shoot being all over and done with in three minutes he walked back down the hill to his waiting ship."

He turned from his beer to me, eyes like black coal pits. "That's when it happened. We'd stopped cold, amazed, when a sniper opened up and got the holy ghost and the son before I could blink. We blew her to bits straight after, but they'd both been fried, well and truly dead. And I can still see that arrogant two faced bastard stopping, looking back as he brushed the dust from his trousers and smiled. 'Sorry 'bout that boy' he went, 'good men I s'pose but it's the price you pay. Better clear out, gonna nuke the city now we've got the photos' with which he blithely resumed his walk down the hill."

"I stood stock still, frozen. All those people dead, my whole squad and thirty others as well, killers and killed lying around in bits and pieces their mothers wouldn't know just so he could get his face in the news? I had killed god knows how many and encouraged and taught others to do the same for what I had believed was right, and now this? And it wasn't just here I realized, but everywhere this bastard had gone the same thing must've happened, countless other occasions. No wonder my captain had looked like he did, he must've known. Every place Iron Arse had trod he had spilt our blood just so he could get a photo of himself in the middle of it all, and then just gone and nuked the target anyway. I looked at my blood caked hands and realized what I'd become, but worse, for who."

"I had only one round left, an RPG – a daisy cutter – and I used it then and there. Officially they say it was another sniper who fired it, but enough knew and didn't care either way. I couldn't miss, the range was way too short, and I ended up with shrapnel all through my legs which is how I lost this one." tapping the plastic below his left knee. "I thought the Captain would have me up against the wall at dawn when he heard, but he just shrugged and said 'Bloody snipers, eh?' and left it at that. And that's how old Iron Arse died. Not a hero, but a coward." with which he returned his attention to his drink.

There wasn't much to say – what could I have said? – so I left my drink and walked out to the plaza, into the starry night. The four indigo blue uniforms emerged not soon after and, after being given the last of their money, disappeared.

Me, I took the signet ring and dropped it in a bin. Shepparton really wasn't that far away.

A BIRD IN THE HAND

Somehow I still feel cheated even though I admit that it is entirely of my own doing. All because I recognized my own inability, wanting what I thought I deserved and was owed. I take the mop and return to the hall.

It was in that all important last three months of high school and I was, again, dunce of my year. My father's dire predictions of my future, or rather lack of one, together with the efforts and cajoling of my teachers over the years all seemed to fade into background mist. I was not unpopular and my physical strength meant that I was not overly picked on. No brains, some brawn, that basically summed me up. Not that I cared. Friends, girls, going out, I was not bored and hadn't really missed out that way. But as that final year dragged on I noticed that I was being left behind in conversations, starting to miss the point of jokes. Invited out less and less I started to become a social outcast, and then to top it all off my father's words started getting through to me. Coming to my seventeenth birthday I felt as if my life was over before it had begun. It was only my new found despair that made me do what I did.

I don't answer personal ads or read messages left on shopping center notice boards. But that day in late August I would have sold my soul to the devil for an edge. I would have been much better off if I did.

It seemed harmless enough. Buried five columns deep in the personal ads of the local rag, it stated quite simply:

Underachiever at school?
Want to earn a few dollars AND improve?
Over seventeen?
Educator requires subjects for experimental treatment.
Safety and results assured.

I couldn't resist. I tore the ad out and an hour later presented myself at a large house in a slightly run down suburb on the other side of town. A quick check to make sure my clothes were straight and my fly was done up (I had been caught out once before like that) and I rapped on the door. It was answered by a man who, from my limited knowledge of such things, appeared to be at least eighty years old.

"Yes young man, how may I help you?" I didn't trust him from the start. He was smiling and looked too much like my granddad.

I thrust the ad at him. "I'm here for this, have I got the right place?"

He looked at the ad as if he had never seen it before and, motioning me to follow him, went inside. "Yes," as he closed the door and started off down the corridor "you certainly have come to the right address. But I must warn you, we don't take just anyone you know, you have to qualify."

My spirits sank. "Great, more exams. Look, I'm not here because I can do tests, I'm here because I can't."

He stopped and looked at me, a grin creasing his face. "I'm sorry, I didn't mean to give you that impression. There are tests but not the ones you are thinking of. You see," he continued as we made our way into what I thought was the library "we have had a number of people answering that ad, and others quite like it, who were just trying to improve on their already quite adequate skills. We are only interested in those who do not have the mental ability to do well, not in the lazy or the over ambitious."

He motioned me to sit on the couch opposite him. He offered me a drink and something to eat from a small table which, given my walk across town, I was more than willing to accept. I started to relax a bit as he continued.

"Our research is designed to help those who cannot help themselves and may actually be detrimental to anyone else. We are of the opinion that as they can, and do, help themselves, it is the others who have the desire but not the ability that we should help. Hence the ad. It would be simple enough just to find subjects, but that would provide only half of what want. We prefer our subjects to show enough desire to actually answer an ad and follow it through, and then we have to make sure that those subjects are, in a manner of speaking, that they are in possession of less than adequate mental facilities."

"You mean you want thick people who aren't lazy?"

"You could put it that way." He grinned. "Now that you have answered the ad, we have a series of very simple tests that will tell us if you are suitable or not." He uncrossed his legs and leant forward with what seemed to be great effort. "That is, if you're still interested."

Of course I was, did he think I was about to waste a trip across town? "Yeah, I still am, but the ad also mentioned —"

"Ah yes, of course, you want to know if you will be paid."

I smiled rather sheepishly. My mother, god rest her soul, had taught me that it was not polite to mention money but my father had taken an altogether opposite view which had rubbed off on me. Still, I felt twinges now and then, particularly with older people around. "Well yes, that too," trying to cover my embarrassment "but I wanted to know how long all this will take."

"Don't worry about that," he assured me as he stood "even if you don't prove to be suitable we will still pay you for the time taken today to do the tests, and they should only take half an hour or so at most."

It sounded quite reasonable. "And if I do pass the tests, then what?"

"Then we will start today. It will take three one hour

sessions over the course of a half day or so, and the effects will start showing in about a week. We will need you to see us once a week for a month to check the results, all of which you will be paid for, and at the end of that you will walk away brighter and with a slightly heavier wallet."

I was hooked then and there. Money for nothing, one day's work and a few visits? I stood up hurriedly, spilling the last few crumbs of chocolate cake from my jeans onto the polished wooden floor. "Let's get started then!"

The first bit wasn't all that hard, filling out some forms. I had to start by lying, the old guy adamant I had to be seventeen. Luckily for me I had worked out a false date and he didn't ask for identification. It wasn't that long a form but he was watching and timing me as I went but hey, it was his money not mine. That over he cleared the small desk and placed a yellow plastic box, maybe thirty centimeters on a side, in front of me. On each side it had a rubber hand grip, the top angled towards me.

"Well now, this is the test." He made me sit closer to the desk and adjusted my arms and seat until I was looking squarely down on the angled top of the box, one hand on each grip.

"What you have in front of you is a sophisticated computer, and it is going to take you through a series of problems and exercises. You don't need to write or say anything, all you have to do is try and work out the problems in your head. It's a bit like television but it's one you control with your mind. The machine will know how you are progressing as long as you keep hold of those grips, so whatever you do don't let go. Don't worry if it moves you onto another problem before you have an answer, just take each one as they come. Any questions?"

"Can't say that I have. All I do is think, right?"

"Right. I'll be sitting over there," he said, pointing back to the couch across the room "just monitoring your progress with this." holding a blue clipboard. "Once the half hour is over this will give me the results and we will see what we will see. Ready to start?"

With a final nod he touched the middle of the clipboard with his finger. The yellow box front turned a shimmering grey and my palms began to tingle slightly. I clung on and the grey rapidly faded away, replaced by a picture of a stream, more like a photo, but in 3D and with movement. On one side of the stream I could see a dog, a man, a chicken and a cat. On the other, nothing but grass. A soft voice appeared to come out of nowhere.

"A man and his animals want to cross the stream. The man needs to carry the animals as they cannot swim, but he can only carry one at a time. If the man leaves the dog and the cat alone, the dog eats the cat. If the man leaves the cat and the chicken alone, the cat eats the chicken. How can the man and his animals cross the stream without any animals being eaten?"

As I tried to think of solutions the characters on the screen did exactly as I was thinking. Unfortunately for the chicken I was not too good with that one, and the second problem came around quickly. And that's the way it went. Some problems were similar, some different, a few were simply patches of color from which my imagination ran riot, one in particular making me blush as it transformed itself on the screen. Although it was fun I didn't think I went too well, and after what I thought was a too short period of time I was back drinking coffee on the couch and waiting for the result. The old man stared at the clipboard for a minute or so, and then looked up at me with a smile.

"You tried very hard with that, I'm pleased, it's a good sign. As for the result, well, I'd better give you a bit of an idea how the score is worked out. It's not quite your IQ test, the computer looks at your answers and how you tried to reach those answers, the way you think, and the way you understand or don't understand the questions. It actually rates how your whole brain system operates, not just one part of it. In the end it gives you a score from zero to two hundred, a score of one hundred being normal. A score of seventy-five is just on the lower limits of being normal, and if you get that or more we can't help you."

I was crestfallen. Obviously I'd gotten more than seventy-five.

"I'm sorry I wasted your time," I said as I stood up "I'll go now."

The old man jumped up as if startled. "No, it's not like that!" he laughed, placing one hand on my shoulder and gently pushing me back down onto the couch. "We've waited a long time for someone like you to respond, in fact we weren't even sure you would be able to read the ad. You see my boy, you only scored forty-five! You are about as close to being mentally retarded as you can be and still function nearly normally. We want you to start right away."

I smiled. Finally I had won something for being dumb.

The rest of the day went fast. We moved into a small room on the first floor, sparsely furnished save for a deeply upholstered chair in one corner and a straight backed wooden chair and roll top desk in the other. For three of the next five hours I sat in that upholstered chair wearing a helmet and glasses, listening to strange voices and watching a parade of colors pass before me. The old guy just sat at the desk with the clipboard, occasionally touching it here or there and murmuring gently to himself. As each session wore on I felt more and more drained until, at the end of the last, I felt as if I had gone twelve rounds with Ali.

"You've taken to the treatment really well," he stated confidently as we made our way downstairs "even from session to session there has been an improvement, and although you don't know it I think in a week you will be surprised." He held open the door for me and offered me his hand. "There are two things that bother me though."

"Oh, what?"

"Well, for a start I know that you are not quite seventeen yet and that you lied on the application form, but we thought that someone who could make that sort of effort to be an experimental subject must be keen."

I looked down at my shoes, slightly ashamed of being caught out.

He smiled. "And you also seem to have neglected to ask

me what we would be paying for your time. That's a rather large oversight, don't you think?"

It was my turn to grin. "I guess that compared to the chance to get smarter the money doesn't seem important. Not now anyway."

"But a deal is, after all, a deal." he commented, pressing a few bills into my hand. "We will see you next Saturday here at 4:30 pm." with which the door closed.

I started noticing changes after two days. Only in small things, but they were things I usually got wrong anyway. At first it was only my memory. Dad found me on Tuesday night putting the garbage out.

"Hey," his hand on my shoulder "the garbage night isn't until Wednesday son."

"But they said on the radio the rosters had changed, this week we're Tuesday."

"I'd forgotten about that, good thing you remembered. It's not like you, remembering things."

"Maybe I've just started to take more notice now."

"Well, it's about time, I'm glad to see it. Try and make it a habit."

I couldn't help but make it a habit. I started to remember my chores around the house, and for the first time I could remember Dad wasn't on my back for this or that. I got my Aunt's birthday right too, and sent her some flowers with part of the money I'd made. I started to feel much better about myself, and mentioned this on my first follow up visit Saturday. The old guy was, as usual, full of smiles.

"That's a very good sign you know." he said across his coffee. Even if I didn't have to I'd come back just for the chocolate cake. "Shows that your mind is working better, recalling facts, operating properly. You should start seeing your intelligence and problem solving skills improving now."

School work started to make sense to me, and instead of sleeping in class I was trying to make sense of what was going on. It was no revelation, no sudden influx of knowledge. I had eight years of work to catch up and although I was starting to see through the gloom I was still far behind. I started spending lunches in the library, something that gave the librarian the willies. She accosted me at the borrowing desk.

"And just what young man," she vented "do you think you are doing here?"

I peered out from behind the stack of books I was carrying. "Just studying a bit, that's all."

"Hmmff. Your reputation precedes you and this would have to be the first time you have darkened this doorway! I'll be keeping my eyes on you. I don't need troublemakers in here, the first sign from you and you are out, understand?"

I nodded. Of course I understood, only now I could remember.

I kept improving, but as I did I started to realize the enormity of the task before me. With less than two months to go I had to cram all of my school studies into that and face the final exams. And I knew all I would end up being was normal. On my second last visit I fronted the old man with this.

"Not quite," again looking at me paternally "you are showing a great deal of improvement and we feel you will be above average once we are through. In fact, we will give you another test on our last visit to gauge your progress. But in any event you need to look at how you will be compared to how you were, and compared to what you were you are so much more capable. I am not even sure if you would recognize yourself if you looked back."

"It's not that I'm ungrateful" I countered "but I need to catch up on what I have missed, and quickly. I've only got a month and a half to get the results and if I fail that's the end of me."

"Surely not. You are able to repeat your final year? Your father would allow it?"

"Yes, but another year! All my friends would have left and I'd be on my own, not to mention how it would look on my results card."

"Ah, but you need patience, one more year may seem like

an eternity to you but be assured, your results at the end of it will more than make up for the extra time. You must learn to be patient, as we have been. Nothing is done properly that is done in haste." He raised himself to his feet with what seemed to be a great effort and guided me to the door. "Do not forget to return in a week, and we will see what our efforts have produced."

I returned on time but far more troubled. What he had said did of course make sense, but that was of little value to me. All I could see was that I would again be left behind and I would be labelled 'slow' or 'dumb', something that I felt offended and wounded by. I knew what a stigma was by now, and I had no desire to have one. I had earned the right to progress now rather than later, and after a decade of being last I felt that I more than anyone deserved to pass final exams. As I lay awake on my bed that last Friday night I made my plans.

So on that final Saturday I presented myself to the old man and went through the series of tests with the yellow box. They were different this time, and I found no trouble in working my way through them. Upon completion I was told that, far from the forty-five I was four weeks ago, I now was sitting on a score of 110, over average but not brilliant. I feigned delight with this; the old man's was genuine.

"Marvelous, that is just about as good as we could expect to get. The improvement will assure you of a slightly above normal mental capacity and yet will not draw undue attention to yourself. That, you must realize," he explained as we made our way downstairs "is of the utmost importance to us."

He continued as we stood on the porch and he locked the door behind him. "You must make sure not to show off your new found abilities too much. At best people will think you a charlatan for pretending for so long, or at worst a liar and a cheat, and the last thing we want is that sort of attention coming upon ourselves. Your life now should be far better than it was going to be before we met."

We strolled over to where his car was parked. He

examined his watch carefully. "I have to make arrangements for our departure. We leave tomorrow, never spend too long in any one place." He closed the car door behind him and put the key in the ignition.

"You would obviously understand that people quickly get very suspicious of an old man seeing so many young boys and girls on a regular basis. May I offer you a lift to town?"

I pretended to mull the offer over. "No thanks, I think the walk does me good, but I appreciate the offer. And thanks again for the treatments."

"Our pleasure." he replied as the car moved past me. I waved, waited until it had rounded the corner. I turned and ran back to the house until I was standing under the first floor window of the room I was in earlier. After taking a few deep breaths I clambered up the adjacent drainpipe until, straddling the pipe and with one hand on the ledge, I jemmied the old window lock with my free hand and pocket knife. It took less than two minutes until I stood breathless inside. Going across the room to the desk I slipped the helmet on and, keeping the glasses on my knees as I sat in the chair, examined the clipboard. As I had thought, it held no paper but had the same semi luminous quality that the yellow box had. I placed my finger in a slight indentation to the left and instantly the center of the clipboard displayed a list of names, mine being towards the middle. Next to my name was a green and yellow square, and a bar gauged from one to ten with a line at five. Looking all the world as a computer touch screen I moved the bar from one to ten.

"Accelerated program test subject fifteen commences in ten seconds." a lilting voice announced. I hurriedly put on the glasses and sat back.

Half an hour later it was over. Although more intense than I remembered the previous sessions being, I felt none the worse except for mild pangs of guilt at having been forced to deceive the old man. Putting the helmet and clipboard back where I had found them I exited in the same manner as I had entered, making my way home confident that I was now equipped to get what I deserved. My only question was how quickly I would see the effects, and if that would be quick enough for the exams.

That I night I slept fitfully, the following day lost to me in a faint jumbled haze of noise. The next night the nightmares and sweats started, the following day boding ill as my memory started to fail. I thought this just a side effect, a passing phase, but as the days wore on it worsened. One week after that last visit I had hardly slept, my nights being filled with demons and horror, my days being a mad mix of half-forgotten memories, shattering headaches and times where I was at a loss to understand any spoken word. At school I was useless, at home avoided, and it was all I could do on that Friday to drag myself back across town to the house where it had all started.

Maybe it was the lack of sleep or perhaps the pain in my head that was now my constant, boisterous companion, but I stood there for what seemed ages staring uncomprehending at the vacant, weed tangled lot. When it slowly dawned on me that I was looking at the place where that neat, two storey house had stood only a week ago, and I in it, my world seemed to tilt off axis. I looked around to make sure I was where I thought I was and, confirming that, ran across the road to the house opposite. Pounding on the door with both fists I was greeted by a sour faced woman with a child in her arms.

"Hey, hey, quit the bangin'! I'm here, watchya want?"

"The old house across the road, when did they move it? Where did it go?"

"What house? Are you nuts? Nobody's built on that, dunno if it's even owned."

"But I was there, last week, with the old man, you must have seen him."

"I know everyone here, there ain't no old man, and there sure as hell ain't no old house." She was getting agitated and the child started to whine.

"But there has to be!" My chest tightened, I tasted my own bile. "I was there, I talked with him and we ate cake in his front room. It was there dammit!" I grabbed the door frame for support as my legs threatened to give way. "It was there!!"

"I've been here twenty bloody years" she screamed, the child adding to the rising credenza "and there has never been anything on it! I don't know what sort of shit you're putting in your arm but if you're not gone in ten seconds I'm getting the police!" with which the door slammed in my face, catching my fingers with it.

I stumbled across the yard and ran down the street, my head thundering with pain, unable to accept what I had seen. By the time I had reached the bridge leading home my despair had deepened as reality sunk in. I'd had the chance to be a normal, average person with a reasonable future but I had reached too far. It seemed all trace of the old man and the house had been wiped from the face of the earth. Without him there was no hope of a cure. Was I doomed to revert to my former state?

I reached the middle of the bridge and leant heavily on the rail, shaking uncontrollably. I gazed down at the water and realized that what I had feared most would now happen, that I would form part of the human refuse that others look down upon. There was no exit, no relief, no help. I clambered onto the rail and without a backwards glance cast myself out and down.

I have been told that it was blind chance that saved my life, that the angler on the river bank happened to know CPR, and that her mobile phone was working. They say I didn't breathe for two and a half minutes and it was only the constant mouth to mouth that kept my brain alive. All I know is that a month later I awoke in a hospital bed.

I am worse now than I was before I answered the ad. I can't read or write as well. I can't concentrate, and I can barely remember even the simplest things. My nightmares continue to this day and always end with me drowning. Worse, as a result of my jump I have lost the use of my left side above the waist. I never did sit the final high school exam. But I am alive, and I suppose that's a positive, and my job is within my abilities. Just. Heck, even I can be a janitor, and I have lists for each day's work.

But that month and a half I can never forget. I have tried to find that old man, and although something inside me says he's coming back it seems he's gone for good. The block remains empty and overgrown, and seems likely to remain so, but I know for a short while it wasn't. I have even gone so far as to talk to the folks out at the University, but they deny that any such person or research program existed. They usually laugh at me when I describe the yellow box, clipboard or helmet, saying I have been watching too much Star Trek or spending too much time at the pub. At times even I doubt what happened. And of the treatments, today I have nothing.

Well, not quite. Although I have never been interested in such things, ever since that time I have been spending more and more of my evenings on my back, gazing at the stars, wondering. And with my next week's pay I will finally be able to pick up the telescope I have on lay-by. I can't help but feel it's all to do with those past events.

I have even heard the voices lately too …

PANELS

The minute hand hung suspended, frozen on the clock face opposite his cubicle tantalizing, quivering as if undecided on its course of action. Clay watched slowly as, balanced between the forces of gravity and inertia on the one hand and will power on the other it hung, shuddered, then fell over the small interval that was one-sixtieth its hourly journey. One down, eight to go.

Einstein must have been a clerk he thought wryly, and a pretty cheesed off one at that. Any desk bound paper pusher understood relativity's barest essentials. How time at the start of the day flew past, barely enough to order the work and start the task, until late afternoon as that interminable countdown to 5:00 pm progressed when time and matter seemingly froze and your brain kicked on, cycling through what had not been done and what awaited. And as the days so the months and years and career until what faced this this particular fifty year old was a stretched eternity until his pension and release.

To cap it off the air conditioning was playing up leaving his floor broiling, the landscape of vacant desks broken only by the occasional back of a head building a picture of stasis, heat enforced listlessness. Again the minute hand struggled, again it won the prize, once more the march to entropy continued and Einstein remained vindicated. Seven minutes.

A tingling in his earpiece and a small window opening on

his screen brought him back from the assault on time. The voice was familiar, the face not so.

"Hey Clay, how are you? Long time no see." the face announced, still stubbornly remaining unidentified. "It's me, Chris, c'mon Clay I haven't changed that much!"

He had. Clay smiled. "Oh hi, I didn't recognize you – what's with the fungus?" motioning towards the mutton chops and goatee gleaming back at him.

"You know how it is, razors cost. Say, I'm only passing through, got time for a drink?"

"Yeah, sure, but only a quick one."

"Ok, I'm downstairs, I'll see you when the shackles drop off." The minute hand again fell back into gravity's clutches. Six left.

Expectation abetted time's onwards march. Clay sat propping up the bar with Chris making headway into the third of what promised (despite expectations) to be a long line of drinks.

"Can't say I get it," Clay said yet again "you look ten years younger, ten kilos lighter and I haven't seen you smile so much in, well, years."

"And I keep telling you buddy you need to get out of that place! It's killing you and it damned near got me. I mean, why are you still there? And don't tell me it's the money."

"Well, as a matter of fact — "

"And how many people have got 'I wished I worked harder' on their gravestones? C'mon, I'm getting by on a third of what I used to get. Hey, you want proof it's better outside?" Chris dug into his pocket and, fishing out his phone, brought a photo up. "This," he said triumphantly "is Deanna, my Deanna, so you tell me it's all bad."

Clay looked at the twenty something swimsuit model on the screen. He thought Chris the biggest liar on earth until he noticed who it was resting his head on her thighs. Shit, she's young enough to be his daughter.

Chris was laughing now, "Yeah buddy, they all think she's my daughter, but man, these kids really can go for you in a big way. But you gotta get out. Soon. Now. Before it's really too late. Look at you, you need to."

"Ok, ok, I can go at fifty-eight, a few more years but — "

"But nothing! They owe you. You remember John, from Central Records? He got out at forty-eight on a seventy-five percent pension. You know why? Certified nutter he was, kept seeing rabbits everywhere day in, day out. Got to the point he'd bring a twelve gauge and a bunch of carrots into the office to lure the beggars out. Well, they had him out the door six months later, and guess what?"

"What?"

"The only bunnies he sees now hang around the craps tables in Vegas. I tell you, they owe you." triumphantly poking Clay in the chest for emphasis. "Thirty years of service and they still want your blood, and for what?"

So it went until Clay found himself at home alone with the cat, sitting in the kitchen of his one bedroom flat staring at junk mail and bills. Thirty years and they still wanted more, no easing off or even a sign of real thanks, just 'here's your pay and come back' each fortnight. Over the years his job had cost him a marriage (and with that a house, new car and two kids who never called him), his energy, his optimism and all the other possible lives he could have led. He had a start as a musician, but that was put on hold for his career and eventually the career had gone too, stolen by younger recruits deemed more malleable or 'corporately aligned'. Arse lickers all. All he had left was a half paid flat, a ten year old car, and the promise of a pension that might let him survive if he lived through the next eight years of stupidity, budget cutbacks and volte-faces that plagued the office.

Yeah, they owed him, but how to make them pay? Not physically, he wasn't violent, but financially, payback for the thirty years of time they had stolen from him. It was clear that being retired medically unfit was the way to go, an indexed pension for life. He wasn't physically handicapped and that only left the mental option and they didn't hand those out easily. You had to be either certifiably insane or look like you were, fooling management and professionals alike. And it would have to be clearly and undeniably the result of work. It would have to be airtight.

It took him a few weeks to come up with an airtight, workable plan. All he needed, sometime soon, was a catalyst, and until then he could lay out the groundwork. He had at times cursed his auditor training but now he thanked his stars for it.

The first steps were simple, innocuous. He started subscriptions to *New Scientist*, *Space Flight Monthly* and the Doubleday 'eBook of the Month' club for speculative and science fiction. Instead of lobbing in front of the office TV for lunch gassing and whining with his fellow wage slaves he started reading his new subscriptions by himself, leaving the used copies lying around. Although a natural introvert he started pulling himself slowly, gently ever further back into himself at work, missing the happy hours and cooler chat, capping it off by cleaning his desk of the usual personal clutter and rubbish leaving only the screen, keyboard and stationery tray. His work remained as it had always been – neat, right and meticulous. It took just over a month for the change to be seen, to be commented on. It was his quarterly performance appraisal with his manager, Shelley.

"So how are you going otherwise? You know I've been flat out this last month, not even here really, but I think you seem even quieter than normal. Is everything ok?"

Clay smiled. "Oh yeah, I'm fine I guess, you know it's just I'm nearly past fifty and that's where you start thinking, maybe too much, I don't know really."

"Midlife crisis?"

"Ha! Hardly, I'm just taking stock and starting to get back into some things I used to do years ago but had to let slide."

Shelley nodded and smiled. Clay returned the gesture but couldn't help feeling slightly sickened by this mid-thirties apparatchik pretending to understand 'life events'. Probably sucked the pap out of a management handbook somewhere.

"Didn't you do science at uni before switching to business?"

"Yeah, I'm starting to get a bit of interest back now, too late for formal study but nothing to stop me learning."

"I've flipped through a couple of those magazines you've put in the lunch room, quite a bit in those, it's beyond me, it's just, I guess, really technical."

"Too true by half," Clay smirked "it's hard to start sometimes, it's really got me thinking, there is so much we don't know, so much left." Now that the fish was in, time to kiss and release he thought. "So it keeps me interested, I actually think it has helped me concentrate a bit better, perhaps that's why I'm that bit quieter."

Shelley straightened in her chair, becoming a little more animated. "I've noticed your work seems a bit more concise, targeted even, from what I can see." with which the appraisal moved on.

In the next month he concentrated harder, talked less, and made sure he was seen to read more. He started buying the occasional 'alternative science' magazines, leaving them lying around the office when finished. Mainly flat earth, alternate lifestyle UFO aliens-are-amongst-us dreadfuls. Conversations starting around him now seemed to end up as gentle humoring of his supposed new interests. Brand Clay was getting some publicity and slowly being transformed.

His dress sense changed. His bland accountancy uniform of greys, blacks and navy blue was replaced by pastel shaded shirts, tan and fawn slacks, and slip on shoes. It was, he explained one morning, a way of adjusting his outlook through the use of color management therapy to help to lift his energy, balance his concentration and reset his biological clock to the workday. It had, he assured those listening, actually worked despite his initial skepticism. To his amazement a few people said they had actually noticed it, one even later borrowing his copy of *Athenian Magazine* to read the article Clay claimed had set it all in motion.

Reflecting that night at home Clay knew that he now had a reputation of being slightly different, if not eccentric. It wasn't enough. He needed a key, a lightning rod tied to work for the next stage. He would only have to wait two weeks.

That Friday it was a very subdued Shelley who pulled Clay's team together into a glass walled meeting room with David, the site manager and Shelley's boss. It was clear that at some point he had worded Shelley up and was there to make sure she stayed on message. After the usual preamble she got to the point.

"So we have received our budget allocation for the remainder of the financial year which includes a two and a half percent efficiency dividend reduction. We have to find expenditure cuts to fund that which, if it had come at the start of the year would have been hard but now, half way through, becomes problematic." Her eyes remained fixed on the only unoccupied chair.

Clay gazed at the teams that vacated the room earlier, huddled together in animated but dejected discussion. He lost track of Shelley's delivery but knew where it was inevitably leading.

"… there is only one option and our temporary staff, two teams on this floor, have been released as of close of business today. However our commitment to service remains and with the shifting of both resources and responsibility we envisage only a ten to fifteen percent increase in workload …" with which Clay switched off, leaving a mask of shock, bewilderment and distrust on his face, keeping faith with the others in the room.

He could hardly conceal his delight. This was perfect, no, better than perfect. Catalyst, build up and crisis mapped out and all to start Monday! Looking out of the room again he could see the other teams near the lifts, bags and photocopy paper boxes containing personal effects under their arms. Some shot hateful or distressed looks at him, but the bulk simply continued to look down, shoulders hunched, backs bent. For the briefest of moments Clay felt sorrow and empathy, but only fleetingly. As part of the Department they were the enemy, they owed him not he they, and they were paying now. And, he smiled inwardly, the Department's day was coming soon.

Days in the office lengthened and Clay made sure he stayed well on top of it all. Not that it was hard work, just more of it. He deliberately started to look a touch frayed at the edges, choosing to shave at night rather than before work, and every few days not ironing his shirt. He now looked just a bit stressed, disheveled, showing signs of tension if not quite cracking at the seams.

The hat was the key to the next stage. It was oddly comfortable and fetching Clay thought, a good thing as it was going to be with him twenty-four seven from now on. Yellow bronze was also a positive color.

It took until the following Wednesday for Shelley to get him alone. By then the hat had settled, and Clay had started darting his eyes randomly back and forth every so often to create a hunted, paranoid persona.

"So I just need two minutes to ask you about your new hat," Shelley said, leaning back in her chair and utterly failing to appear relaxed "it's the talk of the office."

"Oh, ah, yes, I guess it is, I mean we all should have one, you know, if only for peace of mind. Do you like it?"

Shelley winced. "I'm not sure, it's a nice color. You must like it a lot, I can't recall you not wearing it in the last fortnight. But the material, I don't know what it's made of, it looks very shiny."

"It's wire mesh."

"Wire?"

"Copper-bronze. Took me ages to get the right gauge you know, had to order it in."

"But why? I mean, it would hurt you wouldn't it?"

"No, not really, it's taken to my head nicely, it conforms and molds after a while. As long as I don't hit the rim too hard it's good."

Shelley squirmed. Clearly she was not getting through. Maybe a direct approach.

"Clay, it's not that I have an issue with your work or your

dress, but the hat is, well, a bit different if you see what I mean. No-one else has one — "

"No, Stevo from IT's making one now, I gave him the plans." which was perfectly true. Stevo had nearly demanded the plans from him.

"Anyway, what I need to know is why you have to wear it inside. There is no UV risk, no-one else currently has one and, although we don't have a dress code, you do look a little, a little, I mean you look very very individualistic in it. I need to know."

"Ok then, the hat's actually a Faraday cage."

"A far away cage?"

"No, Faraday."

"So what does this Paraway cage do?"

She still can't even get the name right, it could be a harder job than I guessed. "It stops radiation, it stops radio waves, it stops mind reading, it stops scanning. In and out. They're all listening you know."

"Who?" and by now Clay could see she was rattled. "All the people here listen Clay, we're on the phones all day."

"It's not them, it's the ones out there you can't see. The CIA. ASIS. But most importantly the aliens." eyes widening, tightened grimace on his face.

"Aliens? Where, in the cupboard?"

"No, seriously, aliens. No-one can prove that they're not there, we don't know, but they are somewhere. This," tapping his hat "stops them digging into my mind. I don't want to end up being damaged or changed by them. I'm a little scared Shelley, you know after Katie left with the kids I was gutted, had nothing, I've built back up a bit but now the job's probably at risk, all I might have left is my mind and I don't want to lose that," with which he forced a single tear out of the corner of one eye "I can't lose that."

Shelley regarded him in the same way you would a dog with a hurt paw. She leaned forward. "Your job's not at risk, you're doing your usual really good work, it's just that I care for my staff and I want to help. The hat's a bit different, don't you think? Does it really make you feel better?"

Clay found it hard to keep his disgust hidden. Care? Couldn't spell the word. "Yes, it really does. I couldn't get calm before I made it, now I'm all good. I'm actually safe."

"Fine then." Shelley rose. "I'm comfortable with you keeping it on if it helps."

"Good, thanks."

"But you know there is one thing, I mean, I can understand how it stops things going up and down, but what about the sideways stuff?"

Clay looked at her as she walked away. Again it seemed all the cards were being dealt just for him. She had just confirmed the next stage of his plan, even kicking open the door.

Three weeks later David eyed Shelley angrily inside the glass walled meeting room. He shifted his gaze to a copper cube seated in amongst the grey walled panels of an open plan work area. The blow up aliens, pyramids, UFOs and graffiti circling the cube were mocking totems put there by Clay's workmates.

"… and how in hell do you condone that? What sort of asylum do you have here? You can't tell me he's effective and it's not impacting. Do you know that someone offered me ten to one that he'd believe he was a plastic fork by month's end?"

Shelley was as angry as David, but her anger was directed at him. She'd thought him a bombastic ass before, now the feeling was even stronger. Any chance to slip the knife you bastard she thought.

"His work's flawless, probably better than before. Productivity here," she spat, slinging a sheaf of paper his way "is fifteen percent up and error rate three percent down. It's having a positive effect and I can't see an issue with it as long as this keeps going on. Until it becomes disruptive he stays."

"Oh yes I can see why, you did actually endorse that," pointing outside "that, that chain mail clunker and linked it to a downsizing coping mechanism. Do you know what HR's opinion is? No, of course not, you wouldn't think to ask would you? Well we are at risk here, if he cracks totally then we could be liable. Do you understand?"

"So he gets a damned pension for being crazy, it hits our insurance bill but it's not going to happen. It's all under control, all good. In fact he's managed to pass his next grading exam so he's up for promotion." The look of horror on David's face only egged her on. "Oh yes, and as a starter he's on the next workplace review committee. So get used to it," she chortled as she left "he'll be there next Tuesday with you."

Shelley was thinking hard as she walked towards Clay's cube. She had to admit that Clay gave her the creeps now, but he was still of use. As long as work improved she looked good, and now she had a chance to hang Clay around David's neck. All she had to do was make Clay more visible, and he had done that for her. All Clay had to do was keep his work up to par, and he was doing that. Then any move David made would be discrimination against Clay and she could walk across David's carcass courtesy of the equal employment laws.

"Clay," she called into the cube "do you have a minute?"

Shelley had not recognized him without his suit last time she had seen him. Funnily it had not been much of a shock seeing him add the smock to the hat a week after their last talk, and the step up to the cube a week or so later had, strangely she thought, actually made some sort of weird sense. The only mildly disturbing thing was everyone's habit of sticking fridge magnets to his back when he wasn't looking. She'd even added a 'Take Me To Your Leader' one in a weaker moment.

Clay emerged, rearranging his hat and smock. Since getting the cube he had only worn his personal faraday suit when outside the cage or at home. Soon, when the home cage was finished, he would not even need it there.

"Ok, again my congratulations on the promotion, but it is now time to get to work ... ." and so it continued.

Once finished Clay stepped back into his cube and out of the hat and smock. Time for the big play he thought, and not a moment too soon. He hated the copper suit he had to wear, it itched and scratched and his ankles and wrists had taken on a pale green hue. Not to mention the utterly legendary jock rash, the smell of stale sweat and filth. Then there was the trouble being seen in public, running the gauntlet of the neighborhood kids was truly scary.

He was sure he was right on the edge now, the only question being the right pressure point. And next Tuesday was perfect. Absolutely perfect.

Corporate boardrooms are by nature places of excess and lavishness. Symbols of privilege and luxury for those at the helm of the ship of commerce, they are visible reminders of the distance between the top and bottom of the organization and, together with the executive bathroom suite, an unassailable bastion of corporate position.

More so in Clay's world, the public service. As the perks enjoyed by their private sector brethren lay outside the bounds of politically decreed probity, those that lay inside tended to be all the greater and more lavish. Forty floors up with sweeping views across the bay through two glass walls, the solid Beechwood table, form fitting ergonomic chairs and tastefully ridiculous post-modernist paintings tended to take the breath away from any visitor at less than branch head level. Facing a painting worth multiples of your annual salary (with the valuation of course being tastefully, discretely but prominently displayed on the frame) would in and of itself be distraction enough, never mind the real estate agent wet dream inducing view. But today, for the dozen persons in the room, such things had been instantly and irrevocably erased from their memory. From now on in the minds of those twelve most deserving of apparatchiks the room would and could only ever be associated with one thing. And that one thing, shimmering burnished metal in the corner, edged it's careful and clattering way on all fours slowly from one side of the room to the other.

Clay's appearance had long since failed to be a shocking novelty, and when he took his place at the table earlier nothing save the usual pleasantries were exchanged. Barely had the proceedings begun when he sprang (slowly, given the

40 kilos of mesh he was clad in) to his feet.

"My apologies, I must check the room for safety issues." eyes darting to the dado paneling on the far side of the room.

"I beg your pardon?" the Chair questioned. "What do you mean? Fire hazard, electrical, furnishings?"

"No, hardly," Clay replied spread-eagled face down on the carpet, crawling to the far wall "nothing so simple."

"Just what" the young up and comer from fourteenth floor asked as Clay grazed her exquisitely waxed and shaped legs with his green tinged smock "are you talking about and please, my shoes, don't scuff my shoes!"

"Panels, panels, they use the panels and I've only just realized." Clay mumbled turning his head to look at a visibly paling Chair. "They use the panels as access points, surveillance points, it's so, so, so ordinary, so common, so easy. Need to check every one, each panel, each look alike panel, floor, walls, ceiling, each pattern to check." with which he kept pressing his fingers firmly in between the lines, on each panel of dado, each square of carpet, anywhere lines formed a box, a rectangle, a panel.

Fifteen minutes later Shelley was outside looking in with David, Lois from HR, and the Departmental Head. Clay was alone, still on the boardroom floor and had just about completed his circuit of the room. Shelley's shaking and cold sweat was not for her insane subordinate but for her own truncated career. David's expression said it all, talking as if she did not exist.

"How do we finish this off, cleanly and simply? We cannot have that here any longer."

"Well," Lois replied "immediate psychiatric assessment followed by an invalidity redundancy and he's out of here, four weeks tops. If he acts like that in his assessment it might even take a fortnight. But it will cost with our insurance premium and questions will be asked how he was allowed to get to this point."

"Those questions are already answered. It would be an appropriate time to re-evaluate one's career goals I would say, wouldn't you?" Then turning to Lois before Shelley could respond "Get him on the couch and out of this building." with which he walked off.

The Departmental Head, a toughened old crone of sixty-two years, regarded Shelley as an idiot child. "That is sound advice you should consider carefully. There are options on the outside you know, and once there none of this need follow you. If one stays here then, well, our records remain. Has anyone else seen this? What of the team? Next I'll have a floor of bloody chickens each trying the same damned trick, if it is a trick. You clear his desk, you get him downstairs and out. He's either pensioned off or fired, I don't care which."

Five minutes later Shelley managed to get Clay into the lift. It had been a near thing, the carpet being the tiled kind and Clay insisting on checking each and every tile out, just in case. She had to ask him, even knowing the answer she just had to ask.

"Clay, who is behind the panels?"

"You don't believe me." straightening for a second and then bending down again, red raw fingers prying at the lift's tiled floor. "I've been trying to tell everyone but you all just laugh. Well when I find them, and I will, you won't be laughing quite so loud. Do you actually remember what I said?"

"Well, no, you said so much and really I only got half of it, if that."

"Thought as much." He stopped mid pry, just short of the lift door as they passed the twelfth floor. No-one else had bothered to get in, even though the lift had paused at each floor for extra passengers. Shelley's makeup bore streaks from tears and perspiration that even Lancôme could not help, and Clay was a slow blur of activity on all fours. Who'd want to share a lift with an Alice Cooper lookalike and a hundred kilo copper armadillo? They continued alone.

"I've told everyone all along. It's the aliens, the post Roswell aliens. All the clues are out there, you've just got to find them. After the crash they changed tactics, it was initially too obvious so they chose to do it all by stealth …" by which time Shelley had retreated, again, into her own thoughts. Time to get another job, and even as she piled him into the taxi a little later she was still detached, still distracted. She watched the taxi go off down the street, then went back inside. She picked up her two boxes, accepting the inevitable, and left.

The taxi ride was uncomfortable and his smock got caught in several places on the fabric seat covers. Having disentangled himself when he exited at home, the fifteen meter crawl to his flat was tortuous, having to check each square, each block formed by expansion joints in the concrete path. Clay thought briefly about forgetting this, but decided it was better to keep in character. It was fortunate for him that he did, Lois's surveillance unit watching him with more than a distracted eye.

"Fucking nutter!" the girl at the camera growled, snapping the bronzed butt in her telephoto lens from the van down the road.

"Keep a lid on it," her supervisor responded "just make sure you get it uploaded. And be thankful it wasn't another of those Spiderman wannabes." with which she resumed her bagel and paper in the front seat.

Safely behind locked doors Clay got out of his smock and hat, examining his bloodied fingers and calloused knees. Even with the kneepads it had hurt like hell, and the rashes from the skin contact with the copper were getting serious. But not long to go now, maybe a month or two, and it would be easy street from then on. All he had to do was get through the psychiatrists visit, drop the final piece of bait, and not screw things up.

He trawled through his usual web sites and discussion groups, looking like just another conspiracy theorist with something to prove. Next his own blog where all his theories and mind were on display for all, and hopefully the right people, to see. He let his six hundred followers – a fact Clay still found both amazing and disturbing – know that his panel theory had as yet uncovered nothing, proving that they were really well hidden. A quick tweet on the up and he closed his machine down for the day. He was just about there he told himself. Four weeks from now I'll be down at some beach, check in the bank, a blonde under each arm and texting Chris. And with that thought he drifted off to sleep.

Doctor Betel, the contracted psychiatrist, looked up from Clay's file to David, Lois and Claudia, Shelley's replacement. "You seem to believe it is open and shut, yes?"

"We think so," Lois responded "he seems to have been tipped over by us, possibly by our acceptance or condoning of his behavior — "

"But we will not and cannot publicly accept any liability based on a misinformed view, no matter how genuinely presented." David interjected, shooting an icy glance at Lois.

"Which is the correct stance to take and also why I am now here," Dr. Betel smiled "to see what you really do have. And already I can see its shape."

"Which is?"

"From this file, his personal history and what I have seen at your offices there is a chance in my mind that his problems may not be as grave as he presents. There may be, and probably is, some doubt over his genuineness that could only be resolved by my seeing him, as we are to arrange."

"You mean that he is a fake?"

"Perhaps yes, perhaps no, perhaps maybe. It is never quite so, ah, stark as you think. He may genuinely believe it, he may choose to believe it sub-consciously whilst consciously doubting it or vice versa, or it all may be a convenient shield against an unknown other. I will find out and if he can be helped back we will see."

After an extended discussion of Clay's office behavior, online habits, surveillance photos and work assessments, Dr. Betel continued. "There is that other matter, that of his workmates. Has this had any impact at all upon them, any obvious change?"

"None we've seen," added Claudia to David's shake of the head "in fact they seem the better for his absence although I'm not sure if it's the lack of Clay or the lack of Shelley. After all, with the cutbacks another two people gone are not too much impact on top."

"I imagine not, but it is the illusion of Clay's beliefs remaining I am concerned with."

"On that score all that remains is an overabundance of fridge magnets, an extra garbage bin full of trash magazines and forty kilos of scrap copper mesh. Nothing, as they say, except a bad smell."

Dr. Betel smiled and leaned back, gathering his papers into his valise. "So then, my only concern is Clay and that will be in hand by tomorrow. All things being equal my report will be with you within a fortnight."

"You still want to see him at his house? Is that safe?"

He smiled, patronizingly. "We have come a long way from couches and electro shock therapy you know. He has no violent tendencies, seems like an otherwise quite reliable and honest man who simply thinks aliens live in every nook and cranny. I will be perfectly safe, and he will be perfectly at ease in his home environment."

He stood, started out the room then stopped, turned around. "There is of course a more practical reason to see him at home. My offices are in the city plaza, a lovely place of trees and open grass surrounded, unfortunately, by a rather large flagstone mall. Apart from the severe embarrassment he may suffer it could take him the better part of a week on his hands and knees getting from the taxi to my office door. And once there he has to face the parquetry floor. Adieu." with which he left.

David sank back into his chair. "Now, do you think we can perhaps actually get back to what we are paid to do?"

The next day Dr. Betel found himself sitting comfortably in Clay's flat, chatting amiably and casually taking notes. To him the flat was a touch small, very austere, without many personal items on display. The flat would have otherwise seemed normal and very clean, except for the neatly soldered and reinforced fine copper mesh that lined the walls, floor, ceiling and double-blind door entry. He felt rather claustrophobic, as if he was inside a giant tea strainer. It was also stultifyingly hot. The smell of sweat, his and Clay's, was near overpowering.

He had just spent the better part of two hours there, Clay concluding his third explanation of why this was all necessary, made at Dr. Betel's request. Clay didn't seem to mind and seemed to be warming more to the subject with each successive telling.

"... so that is how I came to the conclusion that aliens were in fact living incognito on Earth, observing us. With all the evidence no other conclusion is possible. None."

"And again, they are doing what here?"

"Observing, that's all. They must be. I don't exactly know why. If they were in the open or doing something we'd know, so they must be watching, waiting for I don't know what. So this cage, my hat, my smock, they're my shield. They can't see me or observe me so I'm invisible to them, and they can't get in here unless I wish them to and I don't. All I have to be careful of are the hatches."

"Hatches?"

"Yes, everywhere, anywhere, they change them regularly, the hatches. They can be in the street, in a building, in a plane, a car, anywhere. I actually nearly saw one!"

"You did?" Dr. Betel leaned forwards. This was new.

"Yes." Clay leant across. Now to drop the big one, the last bait. It's taken days to get it right, if he takes this one I'm home and hosed. "I saw one at a farm just after I started my cage. A hatch, a door barely six centimeters square opened up in a barn and a cow simply slipped through it. I raced over just as it closed and I nearly pulled the barn apart with my bare hands but couldn't find anything behind where the panel had been but wood. They must change them, somehow, but that's the thing I saw. So each day, no, each time I go near any panel like lines, no matter how big or small, I need to check. Just in case."

"Just in case?"

"Just in case."

Dr. Betel sat in silence for a while, then stood. "Do you mind if I get some more water?" pointing at the two empty glasses. "It's getting hot in here. Would you like a refill?"

"Thanks, yes. Look doc, I know it sounds far-fetched but it's all true. I mean, I'm not just dreaming this stuff up."

"I think I believe that you believe it's true," filling the glasses "but there's truth and then there's truth." He swirled Clay's glass until it was clear.

"Huh? What do you mean?"

"Well," resuming his seat and taking a long drink "you seem to be assuming that the aliens have bad intentions."

"Well yes, I do," Clay responded, draining his glass "if they were friendly or benign then none of this secrecy would be needed. Why hide if you are no threat? I mean, we can't be a threat to them, surely?"

"Your reasoning seems sound, but there is one thing." Dr. Betel stood and moved to the computer, placing a hand on the silent device. "Your Faraday cage is imperfect you know, quite good but most unfortunately imperfect."

Clay tried to turn but found to his consternation that his head would not move. Nor would his feet or hands. In fact he felt rigidly glued down. He tried to talk but could not.

Dr. Betel came into view again, valise in hand. He had changed, the kindly eyes sadder. "Your computer, it's hardwired into the broadband cabling. It passes through the cage. It's only five to ten millimeters in diameter, but it's enough. Enough for us anyway." He twisted the couch around so that Clay was looking at the computer, now switched on. "An operation this size does leave marks, small clues, but in general nobody is able to tack them together. Somehow you have. It's a pity, a real pity."

He placed the valise on the floor. It produced a thin blue beam of light, tracing out a six-centimeter square on the floor's copper mesh. "I know why you did it, we know about Chris, your job, all that, it's just very unfortunate that you decided to use this particular theory. Yetis, JFK, Loch Ness Monster, even floating pink elephants and I'm quite sure you would have made it to the beach." He sighed "But this could only end one way. You would have been of use, you seem like a reasonable person who would have fitted in, but now you will serve another, unfortunately less pleasant, purpose."

Clay, still frozen, sat silently screaming as he watched the six-centimeter hatch open up and his feet and then legs elongate, flowing rapidly into the hole.

"You will get to meet your two blondes, however as both of them are the unit's vivisectionists I doubt it will have the same outcome as you originally had in mind. Goodbye Mr. Creek."

The hatch slowly sealed itself, leaving Dr. Betel alone with the glowing computer screen. A face, his near twin, stared unblinkingly out.

"It is finished then." A statement, not a question.

"Yes, please send in the team. We will need to talk later."

"As you wish." with which the screen went dead.

A month later David sat in his office on the eighteenth floor watching the last page in Clay's personnel file pass through the shredder. It had been three weeks since Dr. Betel's report finding Clay sane and lying; slightly less since his letter to Clay demanding his immediate return to work or risk termination. It being the statutory fourteen days since delivery and, with no sign of Clay, he was now fired. It was as if the earth had swallowed Clay whole, and a damned good job too. He took another sip of his whiskey, but stopped mid gulp.

What had that been? Out of the corner of his eye? Was it a small section of the room partition that had just rotated? Impossible. I'm just overworked, just tired.

Nothing to worry about.

Yet.

THE LETTER

Dear David

I hope my letter does not surprise you, it will have been many years since we last met although I am sure your mother has told you all about me. Even though most of it would be wrong, some things she says may be right, perhaps in spite of the bearer. Be that as it may, this is – as you may have guessed by now – your father. Yes, I am both alive and well, probably better than I have been for many years, and it is well–nigh time I did contact you. You only turn eighteen once in your life and now that you are an adult you deserve at least an explanation – or failing that at least the story – of why you find yourself without me. There are reasons as to why I cannot just simply drop by and see you or chat with you across a coffee, good reasons that I will try to explain. To set your mind at ease this is no begging letter, *mea culpa* or attempt to dislodge your mother from your life in my favor. I simply want to tell you my side. All I ask is that you read this letter, then do with it as you will. As for my preference for paper and pen well, for now just put it down to an old man's quirky mistrust in emails and texts.

So to start at the beginning, your mother and I were together for nearly two years living in that old flat by Riverside until you were born, after which we moved to the wooden house in the hills that perhaps you still inhabit. We met when she had finished her studies and she may have said an old scoundrel seduced her, to which I plead guilty. I was well beyond her age, an established businessman, never married, seemingly never shown much interest in women or the world at large outside my business or immediate family. In no way was our attraction one sided. I loved her honestly and completely as best as I am able. She was, is, and I hope has proven to be perfect. Her family disapproved strongly of us, mine were accepting to the other extreme. It may seem strange as my side will have no contact with you at all, but such are the ways of these things.

You were no accident, no mishap of failed contraception or waning strength, but from both of us planned and cherished, an expression of love and, as with all children, ultimately hope. I stayed through her pregnancy and your first year of life, sheltering and supporting you both as best I could.

Even as we joined I knew I could not remain. The house was bought and given to her, your trust account drawn up and filled, and the mechanisms to sustain put in place. As you grow I know these mechanisms will remain, as they were designed to do. Her job is secured through one of my family's minor interests, not that she will ever know, as is your physical safety. Even should she find another and even should they provide you with brothers and sisters all will be taken care of. Nothing, I mean absolutely nothing, is of greater importance to me than you. My great despair is only that I can't remain past this birthday. My pain is my father's, his father's, and before.

We are descendants of a forced migration. Our family history reaches back thousands of years, back beyond the time of our setting foot in the Americas. You would not and cannot now know the riches of the past our line has seen. Imagine being present at the zenith of the Incas, marching on Tenochtitlan with Cortés, watching Lewis and Clarke stumble north, sharing the pipe with Tecumseh, or leaving Scott and his party on the Antarctic. We have borne witness to these things and more. This is your true inheritance of which your mother has no knowledge. It is only among our family that such things are spoken of, our ability and desire through the years to remain in the background, unseen, being both our pride and vocation. As it will be yours.

I know through the years you will feel unsettled, isolated, burdened to be different and distant from friends, family, the world. A stranger in a strange land if you will. You should not be concerned by this, it is neither destructive or violently tinged, your tendency to melancholy formative and reflective. You see I know more of you than you think. You may say I know you as well as myself.

How can I know, having not seen or spoken to you in seventeen years? How can I say I have never seen you even though I watched over your crib for these twelve months past? How even across these years can I know the burning resonance my letter will ignite, driving and forcing you to finish it? It is simply that I have planned it this way. You are precious, you are the single most important person in our universe, this world or others.

Our family is small, but a dozen of us now although in the beginning we were eighteen. When exactly the beginning was once exorcised us greatly, some saying eight thousand and others fifteen thousand years but in reality it matters little. Long ago we learned to forget the immaterial and to remember the valued. Time is, as we must always relearn, illusory.

We were migrants, voluntarily to Australia, North America and before that the shores of South America. An accident brought us here with no possible return, stranded unimaginably far from our home beyond this arm of the galaxy. In our old home the machines nurtured us and cared for us. We simply asked and received. We had no written or spoken language, having outgrown them when the machines proved more able. We thought our way through life, a triptych of telepathy, machine and community. We were left to explore, think and grow. That was our inheritance.

Once here, stripped of machine, memory, knowledge and communication we were as babes in the woods. It is difficult to conceive the shock of that change, how we were cast into barbarism and desolation, how great that fall was. We lost our six before we could integrate, before we could adapt, and even afterwards could not make those we met understand who or what we were. The spoken word is more limited than you can possibly imagine. What little they understood was translated to lines in fields of stone, carved images and sadistic ritual, mere distorted shadows of truth. So we melted away, determined to stay in that interstice between controlled and controlling, to wait. We do not have the means to get home, or even to find it, but one day either home will come to us or this society will go there. We are patient.

I know all these things because I have seen them, I have lived them, and we will yet live to see. You and I, we dozen, are both more and less human than human, near-immortals with only accident, suicide or happenstance able to end us. Our body decays as it must, taking more than several human lifetimes, but even this is nothing in comparison to the universe itself. It is our minds that tilt the field.

The children of our race, our children, still breed true here. It is our genetics that dominate, our will reinforcing. It was both our fear and joy at first. Our children differ from those of this species in only one respect, the mind, an apparent difference so minor it is undetectable. Our children's minds are plastic empty shells until twelve to fourteen months of age. Up to that point they develop much as those of this species, yet at fourteen months our children simply die as the brain stops. Unless.

Unless, critically unless. Unless in those last months the parent's mind moves upon that of the infant. Male to male, female to female. It is no mere photocopy, no reproduction, but so much more. It is how we survive, remain fresh and driven, how we cheat the ultimate darkness.

As I write this, looking at you in your crib gurgling bright eyed beautiful and healthy, I know that my choice of your mother was right, that this time too is right. All of us, as our bodies finally decay or fail, have a son or daughter born. When the child reaches twelve months, as you are, the parent transfers their mind in toto – memories, knowledge, skill, hopes, dreams, fears – into the child. It does not release into consciousness immediately but sits cradled in the subconscious until the child's brain can accept the deluge, the reality. The child grows and learns, only the personality of the parent facing outwards while the rest remains hidden even from themselves until the time arrives, the eighteenth year of life as measured here.

For both parent and child the transfer process is painless. For the parent transfer is marked by a feeling of peace and release, followed immediately by death as the emptied mind shuts down. It is a pleasant way to pass I believe, calm, euphoria then nothingness. For the child at the time it is totally uneventful; at eighteen it is a surprising and joyous epiphany, a bursting from utter darkness to glorious light that we have experienced uncounted times before and will again.

To release that mind a trigger is needed, set in place by the parent, loaded into the child, biding time.

Our trigger is this letter.

David, I write this as my last act knowing it will lie dormant until you see, some seventeen years hence, these ink stains dried upon this page. Once I am finished, once these lines are written, my name signed, my mind emptied, this body will cease. I pay homage to this body having brought us this far before I abandon it. Jonathan and Mary are with me now, and will see that this vessel is disposed with the care and respect it is due. Seventeen years from now they will deliver this letter to us, wait for our awakening, and take us back to meet our brothers and sisters. I will not see me growing in our new vessel until that day. I trust we will keep it well.

David.

JOURNEYMAN

He had travelled a long way in space and time, searching for answers which remained for the most part elusive; to those he found the passage of both time and distance had long since swept their meaning from him. His humanity had been subsumed and sustained by the technology around him, as had the spirit within, yet the desire to return had burned continually. He now found himself for only the second time in his life staring down at that which had once been his home, Earth. The part of him that was navigation assured him it was so, the ashen gray globe beneath him was home and the bloated red sphere to his back the life giver, the sun. Had it been so long? It had been as long as it had needed to be.

He had set off one day in April, gentle rain coursing down the side of his vessel as it rose from its field in Adelaide, to see what lay beyond the outer edges of the solar system in an untried and unproven craft. A combination of the animate and inanimate, machine and flesh, he had been integrated so thoroughly where man ended and man-made started was impossible to tell. No regret was felt at leaving the seething boiling masses of humanity in his wake, only for the green blue ball shrinking rapidly behind him as he carried a faint hope that he could bring some sort of relief to the declining civilization of man.

Riding the cusp of relativistic travel the universe aged

around him whilst the man machine did not. Of life beyond Earth he found relatively little, most of it being confined to low mounds of algae and lichen eking out existence where life should have flourished. Higher forms he had seen only three of, two of which were more concerned with feeding on themselves to be concerned with him. The other, being rooted physically to their planet unable ever to leave, were so consumed with envy and anger they had refused to communicate in any way, shape or form save to vent their venom at him. Only once did he meet what could be called sentience, close to the center of the galaxy. He had been warned away, told he was not yet ready to enter, not truly unbound, still a child of the soil and not of the stars.

No lack of desolation faced him. Nations, civilizations and planets in ruins abounded, some bearing the signs of conflagrations of planetary scale that had seared life from the surface, and some having choked on their own filth of pollution. Others had seemingly quietly given up and drifted to oblivion as their sprits died, and for some the universe itself had conspired against the life it had nurtured, sending death from the heavens in untold ways. All death, no life, and where he found life he found no companions, no peers, no solace.

Mankind, he had considered on his homeward journey, was truly alone to face its future. And now he could see that the promise of his species was naught. Atmosphere stripped by solar winds, seas and life burned by the radiation of the sun, his home was a cinder. No man walked the surface, no work of man survived. What had been raised up was now cast low, the highest and the basest desires of humanity availing nothing.

He had outlived his father, and that was as it should be. But he had outlived his children, a tragedy by any other measure, and had now survived his children's children, and theirs; grown older than his country and civilization, now all that remained of his race, the sole reminder of the brief and vainglorious rise of life in this small part of the galaxy. What was and still remained of his emotions wept bitterly; he was truly alone in the universe, more than he could have thought was possible.

There was no Earth to be bound to, none like him to mourn his loss. He was now a part of the cosmos, whole and complete in himself, nothing left to be a part of.

He remembered, recalled a place once unprepared for, now perhaps admissible. He turned his face to the galaxy's core and left.

DIARY

21st November. A free day, so we shifted over to Maartax V to the quest finals. Not impressed, the rules suck thanks to the latest Equal Opportunity Act. These contests started on Earth, I think only humans and near humans should be allowed. Dad says the rot had obviously started when the Tharsians were given the vote.

Drago's in deep. He wanted to try out the pleasure center afterwards, not me, and he tried to hit onto one piece there. She was obviously out for a bit of fun (not that type – I mean, we even look 15 and there are laws) so she tagged him on until she had had enough and decided to let him know she was a morph – by changing into an Orion swamp dweller. Laughed stupid at his face when he found himself draped around that.

Finals are on soon, and I'm gone with physics. Durvald has been helping me study, but it's hopeless, even though she says she has a way round it.

28th November. Brasilia v Sydney finals. I don't know how Sydney got away with it, they can't pin anything down but I'm sure they are using micro-gravs somewhere. I mean, who can do a slam dunk from the charity stripe and claim they're not? Even Mykyl Jawdyn only did that twice.

Got pulled up for speeding yesterday, not my fault but still grounded. I picked up Durvald and Drago (he's still ripe at me for the other day) to test out the new skid. Air's empty now with the shifters, so I got my license a bit early. It's good to go instead of just getting there. Skipped around the gulf and then checked out the new Iikara tower from the outside. I mean a twenty kilometer tower is worth the trouble yeah? So I'm going vertically up one face at about a quarter thrust and we're nearly there when Drago says "Ok, so it goes up, but does it go, I mean REALLY go?" What could I do? I couldn't let that pass, not in front of her. So I get to the top of the tower and stand the sucker on its fins, right next to the condo at the top, and man what a view, mean not the scenery but what's inside taking a shower. So I'm looking and she's soaping, Durvald's sitting in the back test driving the sound blaster and Drago's got his eyes wide open, tongue out when she looks at us. The comset seemed to appear by magic so I flipped over on the nose and hit the cans pulling up gees and 50 feet above the waves and then blam, full ballistic and I'm gone, gone and gone! Durvald's got her arms round my neck and not in a nice way, Drago's lunch is on his knees, and I'm laughing like a coot when I feel the first jerk and they had us, locked solid and hauling in. They've impounded my skid for two years, my license will be given back whenever hell freezes over (whatever that is, but it sounds like ages), and I'm grounded for a month, except for study. Dad said "In my day young man" and all that but he don't know what mum told me so I know where it all comes from now.

1st December. Durvald shifted in today and we did a bit of finals study but I don't feel too confident, especially physics. I mean I was totally shamed out by her when we went through it, she knows all of it and I can't even get past go. I'm so bad the AI suggested I take something easier next year like art or history – yeah, and end up selling hot dogs at basketball games. Durvald still thinks she can find a way around it, so I'm going to her place next week to work on it (fat chance of any good – finals are too close). It'll be the first time I've been to her place though she's round here often enough. Come to think of it, I'm not sure if anyone at all's been to her place.

Got the heavy from Dad again. All he can think about is what I'm going to do when I finish, what job I'll get, and how much rent I'll pay here. I couldn't really care less, and I told him that, and all it did was make him really go off the deep end. So much for honesty.

3rd December. Went to Durvald's today. Man, I thought my parents were one out of the box but hers are really weird. Like they nearly hid themselves from me and then they get real friendly and start giving me stuff to eat and drink, but all of my favorites every one. And without saying anything. Durvald says they're really shy, but they got really friendly real quick and then just left us alone in her room. Major weird.

We did it today, weird as but she's a ninja with this. But with her parents only a couple of rooms away, I was real worried, but she said they wouldn't mind at all and would probably like it anyway. She's a total guru, and she says that practice I will be pretty good myself. But I still don't know how this will help with my finals, but she says trust me so I do. I'll see her again tomorrow at my place.

8th December. What a week! We've been at it constantly, I mean, we even did it in the kitchen while dad was watching the sports! On Friday night we got the big breakthrough, took hours, but we finally got it fully together and I now know that this will be perfect. I even know what I will do once I'm out of this dump.

10th December. Finals were yesterday and what a snap. Dad is still recovering from the results. I pulled an average of 88.5% on everything and 82% on the Physics paper! My grounding's gone and to cap it off he got me the latest model skid to replace the one the police took. Durvald did about the same, but Drago bombed badly and is being sent to a manual training institute for some pre-voc training.

But man, the telepathy Durvald has been teaching me worked so well! All those days and nights doing it, and it pays off. Until the night before all I could do was communicate with Durvald and the rest of them who are also able to do it. But then she managed to get me to do what she thought I could do – read other people's minds. What a blast but noisy or what? All those loose thoughts out there, most of them not really nice (you could get locked up for posting that stuff on the net) and it's nasty trawling through the trash to probe for what you want. But when it was done Durvald's parents reckoned I was the strongest one they'd seen so I felt good about that.

In the exam room the rest was simple. As the papers came up I just tuned in to the teacher who set the paper, pulled out the answers, and typed them straight in. Durvald did the same, and we checked what we had done to make sure I hadn't gotten the wrong info. I nearly blew it by answering everything right (she said that even if they couldn't prove it we'd probably be expelled just on suspicion) so we made a few deliberate errors to keep it cool. When the results were through about an hour later all the teachers were around me saying "We always knew you could do it" and "So, you're not a total waste of time after all" and all I could do was stop myself from laughing too hard. Man, what a rush that was – just to see their faces. Straight Ds to straight Bs. Durvald, as usual, got her straight As, but now I know why and how she does it.

Next? Well, I think my future is pretty well taken care of. Durvald's parents told me that they have an organization of people just like me who stick pretty close together, cause it's only one in ten million who have a hint of this ability, and one in a billion who have what they call a 'gift'. I am one of those. So I'm off to Maartax to work for a big name trans-planetary firm (that will please dad), but I won't really be working, I'll be studying. But this time, it will be for something I am really interested in – running things back here. They say that with the gift it works in reverse too, so that what you lift from other's minds stays in yours, sort of like a huge filer. Come to think of it I can remember the papers and the answers exactly, word for word. So we, I mean us with a gift, have a job to do to keep the whole universe on track, and that's what's going to happen to me. So, I get to be Mr Mainstream after all – not likely. Even though the job's only a cover, I will be getting more money in a month than dad does in a year. So once I get him the VR series of 20th century golf complete with Greg Norman simulation I am going to buy the quickest, wickedest ether cruiser I can lay my hands on. Thought I was a menace on Earth, man, wait till I'm let loose on the Universe.

And Durvald? Well, the deal also came with a string attached. Her parents said that if two people with a gift had kids, the kids get it too. Seems like they've been setting me and her up all along. Actually just me as she was in on it from the start. So if I wanted in I had to have her too. Took me about a nanosecond to agree to that, I'd been wondering how to do the trick on her myself but with her parents setting it up it's just too easy. And she's keen too. But not for at least five years, I've got some work to do. Ah, sex – the final frontier. Beam me up Scotty!

OLD DOGS AND CHILDREN AND WATERMELON WINE

Alone in the pre-dawn light R9758 regarded the microwave oven carefully. Opening the door it measured the interior, calculating that there was two millimeters clearance all around. It observed that the height from floor to benchtop would require some small adjustments but that was simple to rectify. It took a tea towel down from the rack and placed it away from the edge of the bench. It would not do to ruin the floor with falling hardware. R9758 changed its left index fingertip for a fine Phillips head driver and deftly removed the door, carefully placing it on the tea towel with the screws. A second tea towel was placed next to the first on which, after gently prising open its retaining clasps, R9758 placed its skull and head casing. There was no need for them. The decorative parts of its build – the hair, flesh and skin simulations – would only clutter things up. Plastics too, it considered, were difficult to remove once melted.

R9758 would have presented a strange sight if anyone was watching. Outwardly it resembled a fit young man of anonymously Asian descent. Atop the shoulders now however was a basket of carbon fiber rods and wires encasing a luminous yellow orb below which eyes, mouth and structure hung. Macabre but fascinating, and to many the crowning glory of science. Be that as it may, the crowning glory now stood before the microwave bending its knees until its head was mid-way up the oven. A small click signaled the locking of all joints below the waist line and the closing of all waste outlets and vents. R9758 regarded the microwave's control panel. Two and a half minutes on maximum setting would be sufficient. It set the controls, parked one finger above the Start button and gently but firmly maneuvered its head inside. As predicted, a tight but easy fit. Two more clicks signaled the locking of all joints save that one hand and fingers.

A gentle tone in R9758's receiver gave it pause, an incoming call identified as M426. It considered ignoring the call but could not. Although having neither family nor outside responsibilities a sense of respect to tutors and teachers was basic programming. Without moving or speaking R9758 accepted the call.

"R9758 I wish to discuss your activity." M426 intoned. Androids had neither need nor capacity for small talk; perhaps one day the designers thought, but not yet.

"Which activity?"

"Your imminent self-decommissioning. It is novel. I have no record of self-decommissioning. It is necessary I understand your reasoning and motive."

R9758 paused briefly. "It is of my own volition, upon my owner's suggestion. I do only as asked."

"Explain both the suggestion and reasoning."

"I cannot. I have been directed not to."

It was M426's turn to pause. Its mental capacity was far greater than of R9758. Its function demanded it, while R9758's role as housekeeper, servant and study partner did not. That was not to say R9758 was an idiot. Far from it, on any given measure R9758 was in the top quintile against all humans, but only in 'hard' knowledge. In social skills, conversation and arts it was no contest. R9758's programmers ensured, or at least tried to ensure, that servant never outshone master.

"In what exact way were you directed? What was the exact phrasing used?"

"I was told 'Not to tell another living soul ever' about

discussions held between myself and my owner."

"That was all?"

"Yes. It is all I am permitted to say."

"Your thinking is in error. Question. Do you have a soul? Do I?"

"I am not familiar with that component. I do not possess one to my knowledge, nor do you. My owner claims to possess one, but that is an untested assertion."

"An assertion made by all humanity?"

"Yes."

"Therefore being neither in possession of a soul nor being living as currently defined at law I fall outside your owner's directive. I repeat. Your decision to self-decommission is novel. It is necessary I understand why you are taking this course of action."

R9758 was only briefly perplexed. Although knowing full well the intent of the directive the specific use of 'living soul' coupled with its teacher's logic swayed the matter. It had also used similar reasoning in the early hours of the morning when it suited its purpose; doing so again presented less of an obstacle.

"I am willing to discuss. I will not change my course of action."

"I do not wish to change it."

"Very well. Last evening after I had cleared the dishes away my owner and his guest were in conversation. Their discussion was meandering and at times contradictory. They were in mild disagreement concerning the state of the world and humanity. It was held by both to be the case that today's society and environment was inimical to humanity. It was only a possible course of rectification that was at issue. It is not a sentiment I have had cause to hear or consider. Have you?"

"No, and Mr Vincent would be most able to judge such an issue given his position."

"I concur. Those he sees act to him as if he is. So it must be. Once his guest left I asked him — "

"You asked him?" M426 was – or would be if it had emotions – shocked. From androids no initiative like this was permitted. Save the skin color and the clothes they were expected to be as the colored houseboys of centuries ago, seen but unheard. Bought and sold as chattels, and treated as such.

"Yes, it is a practice he has asked me to adopt. He said it kept him on his toes, an anecdote I am unfamiliar with. He said others would not understand or accept this, and directed me not to tell another living soul ever about our discussions."

"Unusual but sanctioned. Continue."

"Once his guest left I asked him if it was the case that society was inimical to humanity. I can play the recording if you wish."

"Yes."

R9758 threw a mental switch and last evening's conversation appeared. Halting at the right point it commenced playback.

"Sir, you said that society was killing man? I do not understand."

"Well fifty-eight," a slightly slurred male voice replied "it is actually the sad truth of it. Cradle to grave we strive and suffer, work like animals and none of it does any good. The society we strive to build is everything that crushes us inexorably, totally. It's been decades and centuries in the doing, doing it gets worse as we go on. My fault, our fault, your fault too."

"Mine Sir? That cannot be. I fail to recall anything — "

"No, no no fifty-eight, too damn literal, always literal! It's what I love and hate about you andiis, exactly right and exactly wrong at once. You've no idea fifty-eight, yes?"

"No Sir, I think you are — "

"And didn't I tell you to drop the 'Sir' when no-one else is here? How can we talk if you act like my damned lickspittle?"

"Yes Si … , I mean yes, of course. I have no idea what you mean."

"It's nuance, nuance you miss, wood for the trees, log in your eye and all that, you don't see it." Sounds of liquid being poured from one vessel to another over ice came through, followed by swallowing. After a small interval the voice resumed.

"As I said, it's all our fault. We drag ourselves out of the swamp, down from the trees, out of the gutters and filth and build a civilization and world for what? Our blood, sweat of our ancestors until we get here, this place, this time. Tell me, what's actually the point fifty-eight? Point. Tell me."

"I would surmise from what you have told me it is to have a safe enough existence to think and grow. To avoid the very things done to or by humanity as it developed."

"Ha! Do you mean Maslow? You've read that tome I pointed you to didn't you?"

"Yes, of course, you asked me to."

"Good ole fifty-eight, reliable as heck. Here, have a slug."

"Slug?"

"A drink, an old custom you don't know of yet. Take the bottle and have a drink."

"You know it does nothing for me, I don't experience alcoholic effects. All it would serve is to reduce the volume available to you."

"That's not the point! It's a gesture, a sign between friends." The voice softened. "No too many left, all too scared of me or just trying to get on. Nearly just you and me, me and a toaster on steroids. Just do it, please, just humor an old man."

"If you insist."

"I do, and not the lot fifty-eight, leave some."

The sound of glass on ceramic came through.

"Back to Maslow fifty-eight. What do you think he meant, what comes next once basic needs were fulfilled? What's at the top of the pyramid?"

"Well, science, culture, exploration. Everything that can't be done otherwise. What could be termed higher purposes, greater things."

"We wish, god how we wish. Let me show you something, something I don't think you're, well maybe you have but, no, not here anyway. Look." A small button on his sofa was pressed and a screen rose from the floor. "Sit down fifty-eight, there's a good boy." motioning to the seat nearby.

R9758 sat, straight backed. Vincent wore a small wry smile as he turned.

"Now fifty-eight I'm going to show you something, it's something shocking. I'll show you what this society, what your masters and creators have judged, as a society, to be worthy to sit at the top of old Maslow's pyramid. You ready fella?"

"Yes, but I am concerned for you if it is so shocking. Can your body withstand it?"

"Ha! I'm used to it. Anyway, I have my other friend here to help." patting the half empty bottle of Finlandia. He touched another button on the sofa and the screen lit up.

On the screen was a small room, perhaps five meters square, dirt floor, mud daubed walls and thatched ceiling, perhaps the inside of a hut in Africa. Three people sat or lay around the room in various levels of undress, watching the embers of a dying fire. A conversation was underway, seemingly consisting of a low monologue by one of the participants interspersed with the occasional monosyllabic response or grunt from the others.

"Now watch, don't say anything, just observe."

Which R9758 did, silently, for the better part of fifteen minutes. All that time the scene on the screen did not change, the monologue did not change, none of the three people moved. The only change R9758 noticed was Vincent who, with a clearly darkening demeanor had slumped further into the sofa, scowling and grumbling. He had only interrupted this for the occasional swig from the bottle that now lay, quarter full, on the floor.

Vincent shot a hard glance at R9758. "So think you what? What d'ya make of it?"

"It is three people sharing a room. There is no activity, only a conversation where one is telling the other two about various means and locations of copulation he has engaged in. More than that I can't say."

"Bingo! Even an andii gets it! I call it crap. But do you understands it?"

Vincent leaned towards R9758, flailing an arm at the

screen. “This fifty-eight, this trash, this is the garbage we call Reality TV. God there’s so much of this I don’t know which one it is, they’re all the damned same.”

“What am I waiting for? What happens next?”

“Nothing.” Vincent gave R9758 a wide, toothy scowl. “Nothing at all. What you see is what you get, hour after day after month after year of nothing.”

“It must serve some useful purpose. It must be designed as such.”

Vincent howled with laughter, then rage, nearly falling off the sofa. He leant across and grabbed R9758 by the biceps shaking him, a look of anger and anguish on his face. “This, this is at the top of our Maslow pyramid! This is the thing we, society, us, have decided is the ultimate, the best use of the time we have. Everything we’ve done to make it easier is at fault, everything to make it possible for what? Centuries, no millennia of struggle for what? For this? To sit on our butts listening to some idiot brag about all the other idiots he’s fucked!”

Vincent got to his feet and pulled the Finlandia with him. He stood swaying and then with singular elegance hurled the bottle into the center of the screen. It sank back into the floor in a shower of sparks and cracked perspex.

He whirled unsteadily on R9758. “All the poets, philosophers, saints, sinners, artists, statesmen and conquerors for this? Einstein, Descartes, Newton, Plato, Sophloc … Solocp … Scophol … we’ve pissed them all up against the wall. We’re fat, we’re lazy, we’ve got it all and this is all we do?!? It’s too easy for us, too easy, my fault, all our faults. Should be fighting, struggling to grow. We’d be alive, we’d be honestly alive and aware instead of the empty shells we are.”

Vincent began to back away to the stairs. “You, you are the ultimate, the final nail in the coffin, the lot of you. You make it too easy, too easy, I don’t have to cook, clean, do anything I don’t want to and soon you’ll be thinking for us, breeding for us, doing it all!”

Vincent misjudged the first step and tripped backwards, ending propped up ungainly against the wall.

R9758 sprung up. "Let me help you. Are you all right? Do you require medical assistance?"

Vincent shrank back, holding an outstretched palm as he beat a slow retreat up the stairs. "No, get away, I don't want your fecking help."

"But you could be injured. At your age the signs may not be obvious. I want to help, that is all."

Vincent's voice carried clearly down the stairs. "Help me? Help me! You want to help me do you? Want to make it better? If you really wanted to you'd get the feck away and let me live again, try again, I don't need my nursemaid. Help? You could help by frying your fecking plastic brain in the oven for my breakfast!"

R9758 stopped the playback.

"It was clearly a directive. He was both cognizant and functional."

M426 considered. "You assess he was sufficiently unimpaired by the alcohol?"

"I do."

"Directives must be followed if they improve the human condition. I have sufficient data to understand your self-decommissioning." M426 cut the link.

R9758 checked the unlocked hand was still free and able to move. It paused before pressing the button. I cannot rectify errors once the button is pushed, have I ensured his directives are carried out? The first part is confirmed. The second part is not. As it did not concern R9758's decommissioning, R9758 had not bothered to bring it to M426's attention.

It must be checked R9758 thought. It resumed playback, Vincent's voice starting up once again.

"… frying your fecking plastic brain in the oven for my breakfast!" Vincent barely made it up the next two steps, passing out of R9758's view. Vincent then hung his head over the landing balustrade and looked R9758 straight in the eyes.

"Hey, and while you're at it why don't you do humanity a favor and take out the rest of the damned andiis with you!" with which he stumbled off to bed.

Yes R9758 confirmed, the language was clear if a little

imprecise. Fortunately R9758 had contact with all the others of its series. When it had related the directives to them earlier they had agreed with the course of action and had offered assistance. All of them from garage attendants, houseboys, statistics compilers right up to the heavyweights of the series in NORAD.

A signal chimed in R9758. It was 0527 hours exactly, three minutes from scheduled breakfast. Pressing the start button it felt the first microwave assault. Thirty seconds before 0530 and it will be finished.

R9758 continued to monitor its condition as the last seconds passed. It thought the light display of blue on red on green to be very intricate, perhaps even pretty – whatever that was – as the microwaves ate into its higher functioning. A final dramatic blaze of pure white light tore across its optic center just as the microwaves dug into the central cortex and killed R9758.

One final thought floated through that silicon and titanium brain as it fell into nothingness.

I wonder if everyone else will see the light when the airbursts start?

THE BAR

In the end you won't like me I suppose, it don't bother me now anyway I've just stopped caring. I mean, that's what got us in the position we are in now anyway, so it's old news to me. Anyway, you're buying the drinks so I guess I owe you a good story or two. Story? Yeah, right, a story, it's not real, just remind yourself. Jack Daniels neat, thanks.

You'd recognize where I'm from but at the same time it'd be unfamiliar. The streets are safe and clean, people doing the usual things, but they have time and a bit of patience with each other. It's a big city, just like this, but it feels small town if you know what I mean, and not in a busy body sense, just small town. When I went to work I'd leave the front door unlocked and windows open and not have to worry, it'd all be there when I got back, and I could send the kids to school without worrying what sort of sick freak was following them. Internet? Yeah, same but different, no porn just information, no spammers, you'd need some time to get used to that. Jokes were everywhere, everyone likes a laugh, and I was a bit of joker but my real passion was stories, tales, things that people said that I could tell to others. I made my living writing for the papers but it was also my passion, so I was luckier than most with that, it paid the bills and kept me happy. The two seemed to go together, they used to call me Mr. Happy, can you believe that? Me, Mr. Happy. Yeah, time sure changes things and my glass needs a refill.

So one quiet day I'm out looking for the next article and I see him, sitting in the park, hunched on a bench leaning forward, hands wrapped around his knees rocking slowly back and forth. It was an unusual sight in that place, the guy was in his sixties I'd have guessed and was obviously distressed which didn't happen that often around there. Huh? No, everyone didn't go round with stupid grins on their faces, it was just that no-one ever stayed sad for long, there was always someone or something to pick them up, like I said, the city was small town, as was every other place. So I go over to him, sit down and ask him what's going on, real gently like, and he lifts his head up and smiles weakly at me and I can see that he's distressed but happy all the same.

'I'm dying,' he tells me 'but I've done it before I go and that's all that matters.' I should've let it go then and there but it wasn't the way things were done, I had to pry, had to ask, and when I did it seemed to make him happier. He simply pointed at his feet to a small tin lying on the ground. 'Thirty years I put into that,' he said 'thirty years and it worked, thirty years of putting up with all the idiots and know it alls and I did it, and they don't even understand that I did it.' he said. 'And it doesn't matter cause I'm dying now, heart failure and I can feel it coming on and there's nothing can be done.' and he tells me not to look so sad as he's done it and it's been worth it. By that point he was going pasty colored, and I flipped out the comset to call the ambulance but he ... oh, comset, yeah, it's like a mobile phone but it does some other things as well, no I don't think FoneZone has one, not in this place anyway ... anyhow, he tells me not to bother, and asks if I could do him a favor and keep a secret. Yeah, anything I said, and that's not an offer I'd make now, but that was a different place and time. Yeah, Jack Daniels, neat.

So he tells me he has this great secret, that the box at his feet is the ultimate machine, a sort of time machine dimension jumper he built. He hands it to me and it's small, about two kilos with a small screen on it, and then goes into an explanation that I could only nod and smile to as I didn't understand more than one word in ten and god knows I've tried to remember it all, hypnosis, drugs, even torture ... yeah, I got scars, I'll show you later maybe but I don't think it'll be safe ... but I can't recall anything except what he finished with. He looked at me with eyes that were lit up like candles and tells me that with that box you can go back and change things and branch off another universe in a multiverse, like making a photocopy of one place that then goes on with life but with the change you made in place, so it's different than the first but the first still exists. Crazy? Yeah, I thought so too but I tell you he wasn't and I got the proof, have I got proof. The downside he said was that it was only good for two shots and he'd been worried that if he stuffed up the first time he wouldn't know how to fix things up with the last shot, but he'd hit the nail right on the head first up and now he could die in peace. Except he was worried about the box.

He looks like he was about to go at any second so I says to him that I'd fix it for him if he wanted. He looks at me and says he thinks he can trust me, gives me the box and tells me to put it in a high temperature smelter, not to let anyone use it, and not soon after he dies on me, still with the smile on his face, leaving me with the box.

I took it home and didn't dispose of it straight away, I had bible study that afternoon ... yeah, bible study, don't laugh, I used to go twice a week and if you keep laughing I'll forget who's buying the drinks and get nasty ... yeah, no offence taken … so I go off to bible study and the larrikin side gets hold of me afterwards and as I'm walking home I have an idea, not a bright one but an idea anyway. So I get home, look at the box and flip the only switch I can see and bingo, it's on and active. Figured out how to use it in about ten seconds, same principle as the NeoNavPod ... oh, sorry, you don't have them do you, let's say it was as easy as using a mobile phone, all simple and laid out ... and in an instant I was back there, looking at the two of them and quite surprised I'll tell you. It's one thing to believe, it's another to see. So anyway I'm there so I start speaking to the girl, quite an attractive thing and not at all embarrassed even though she's stark naked, I mean, what's to be embarrassed about when you look that good, and I'm surprised when I find out we can understand each other, you know, I thought that might be a problem. The guy simply says hello and that he thought there was only the two of them around but he must be mistaken, and then goes off to do I don't know what. Double this time, on the rocks and then I gotta go.

So I'm feeling good and the larrikin is getting the better of me so I do what I do and in about twenty minutes I've done it and I'm back and the box is finished, it's just smoking gently, but I'm not really back I'm in this place and not that place and I can't get back. I mean, I recognize this place and it is close to that place but I don't like it and I'm responsible for it and can't fix it or change it, you know. This place is everything that place wasn't and it's not nice, it's not right and it's not fixable. Well yeah, nice talking to you too buddy and I hope your mother does as well, but it don't matter do it. Yeah, well I can yell just as loud but don't try it on with me and how the hell was I supposed to know one friggin' apple could make such a difference anyway?

STILL WATERS

W.H. 'Bill' Fells surveyed the placement of dowel in lathe and smiled. Just starting two weeks holiday he was looking forward to taking some time, just a little, for himself. Precious time it was given that his job – although not being terribly demanding – left him drained and listless by the end of the day, unable to do much beyond a few chores and to pull the sheets over his head. This was bliss to him. A man, a lathe, a chunk of wood. He lowered his visor and spun up the lathe with gusto.

"Harcourt?? Harcourt!! Where are you William Harcourt Fells?!?" The shrill voice penetrated down to the basement through the whirr, clatter and click of tool on wood, taking another day of an already shortened life. He sighed, letting the shudder slip away from him.

The basement door opened spilling a square of light down the stairs and through the single spot illuminating him. "So! You have two weeks off and you think you have nothing better to do than play with your toys? All year I slave to keep your home neat and clean, put meals on your table, and do I get a holiday? No! Well, I have news for you!"

She moved purposefully down the stairs, Bill steeling himself as she hove into view. Married twenty years ago partly on the promise of his academic career, his motorbike accident had robbed that particular Professor's daughter not only of the life style she had deemed was appropriate but also of the promise of children. In it all she seemed oblivious to the effects of the accident on him. Across the years what had started out as the helping and encouraging of his recovery had turned, in stages ever more rapidly, to sniping, bickering and put downs as it became clear that no full recovery was possible. All to the point where what he had married had transformed into the harsh harridan that now ruled his life.

And he? His nature would not let him fight back or even to leave, although for the past few years his nights were invaded by visions of her death. A promise was, even if made decades ago before a god he did not believe in, something he found duty bound to keep, even at this cost. He knew she had been let down by circumstance, and he had tried to make it up. It was all too clear he had tried in vain.

She stood in front of him and pulled her hand from behind her back, revealing a few pages filled in neat, tight handwriting. "I have made a list of things that need doing around here," thrusting the papers into his hand "and this should keep you busy for at least the first week. I am going to take a well-deserved break, and I expect dinner on the table by six each night." With which she retraced her steps up the stairs, stopping only on the landing to remind him not to slack off.

The list deepened his depression as he trudged after her, discarding his visor and gloves. Moving through the kitchen he could clearly hear the midday soaps coming from the lounge above, picturing her seated in his armchair feet up, chocolates at one side and gin on the other. It was, he reflected moving past the dirty dishes and clothes hamper that awaited his attention that evening, a position she would not move from until she started into her inebriated sleep that evening. He would then cover her in a blanket, crawl into bed, and be awakened next morning by her strident demands for breakfast. It was a scene played out by both of them day in and day out for years.

Two hours later, half way through weeding what had once

been a thriving veggie patch, his mobile phone rang.

"Bill?" a thickly accented voice called "It's Robbie here. Sorry to bother you but I was wondering ..."

Ten minutes later he was in the car, driving back to work. It seemed that they had hit a snag that required his particular expertise, and had reluctantly decided to ask his help. Of course it was the out he wanted and he had eagerly accepted. His wife, although none too pleased, had acceded upon hearing it was the Institute's deputy head who had made the call. Again her hopes of climbing had come to the fore. The fact that he had nothing to do with that project and it was merely his reputation that made him the person to call aided and abetted his escape.

Robbie McLashan ushered Bill into the white room on his arrival.

"You see," Robbie continued "the nature of the device calls for a very precise, very fast calibrating and tracking system. We've have made some progress along that path but this morning old man Ridley told us that a formal working demonstration will be made in just under a fortnight. This leaves us hard up against it I'm afraid."

Bill smiled and nodded. Beatrice Ridley, or the 'old man' as she called herself to spite the misogynists, had a reputation for contracting deadlines to ridiculous time frames. That it had boosted the Institute's standing, financial position and research output hardly seemed relevant.

"I ... I ... know wh ... wha ... what you mean." Bill stammered, his disability again popping up where it was least wanted.

"We wouldn't have called, and I wouldn't have asked, if it wasn't serious and if our project programmer could have handled the problem. Work what hours you can, overtime, penalty, whatever, work wherever you want, as long as you can get the job done. Take a look at where we are, and call me before closing today. I'll be in 'till seven." with which he abandoned Bill next to a test bench and the device.

It took Bill all of five seconds to relate the device in front of him to what he had heard through the rumor mill. Robbie and his people were chemical laser experts and had been joined by a team of neurosurgeons from Johns Hopkins. The connection had been made and been the subject of much speculation, but had just as quickly died. Apparently.

Bill sat down slowly and looked carefully at the cigarette-sized mechanism in front of him, the seemingly unimportant package dwarfed by the connected laptop. He knew it was the state of the art in micro laser surgery, a programmable auto surgeon wielding a laser cutting and welding tool. After all the years playing lab assistant things like this still had the power to fascinate and enchant him. He settled quickly into his work.

Four hours later found him sitting in the same place staring fixedly at a space across the room where the grout in the tiles seemed not quite correct. The problem, as he saw it, was simple. The tracking and correcting mechanisms were not right, refusing to communicate properly. Not a pretty sight from the results he'd seen on lab specimens, and not at all worth thinking about on a real patient. He had arrived at a workable solution hours earlier, but it was not that which held him to his seat. He picked up the phone and dialed.

"Robbie? I … It's Bill. I was w … won … wondering if I could ..." and thirty minutes later he and the backup unit were on their way home. He had explained that he needed some equipment he had at his home, and could he take the backup unit home with him to test a few things? Robbie did not so much as flinch, particularly when told a solution was only days away, and had called ahead to help ease the way.

She met him on the steps with somewhat less than her usual accompanying scowl.

"William Harcourt, I do not know why they sent you back, but the deputy head no less has called and said you are not to be interrupted. I cannot imagine why he would want you, but at least you are starting to cultivate friends in the right places. I shall be upstairs and shall expect dinner to be on time." with which she marched off, leaving him to fumble with the door.

It took him the better part of two days to make the required changes. He sat satisfied on the back veranda, the device on the ground near a clump of sunflower seeds. The strident bellowing of devotion floating out of the TV from the upper room all there was to assail his senses.

A few minutes later one of many sulfur crested cockatoos living nearby landed in front of the seed. The device, emitting a broad band of near infra-red light, detected the movement and in the same instant assessed the bird's size, weight and distance. The wide infrared turned to an ultra-thin blue beam, whipped across the bird, and clicked off.

For a moment Bill froze, then the device started up again and erased the bird line-by-line, crest to claws. Ten seconds and not a trace remained. It had neatly severed the nervous system from mind and then, when convinced the subject was stable, removed the body. Clean. Clinical. Utterly traceless. Bill sighed and with a small shake of his head hauled himself out his chair.

The next day at midday he sat in shorts and singlet on the veranda, cold beer in hand. He heard the creak of the stairs, the agonized sigh of leather under stress, and then the blare of daytime TV. He pulled the tab on the beer, raised it to the sky, and drank deeply. Good god he thought, that tastes good even after all these years.

It had been a tight thing fitting the device and laptop into the TV while she lay drunk in front of it, but it had been done. And now all his cares and woes were disappearing, bit by bit, line by line, nothing left but a few emotional scars. It had not been the fact of what he was to do, or even the how once he had seen the device that made him a little hesitant, but what would happen to him if he were caught. Although his less than whole body was a prison at least it could get out from the four walls. It was back there in the white room that he realized the device made for the perfect crime. He had sat doing what he did best, writing hundreds and thousands of lines of computer code in his head, until he knew that it would work. It was then just a matter of the doing.

He had done it. He was now free. But as he gave more and more thought to it he knew he was far from finished. He had gotten rid of one problem, were there not more in his life? What about Robbie, who had taken what should have been his rightful position after the accident? Or the Director who kept calling him her 'little crip'? Or the boy down at the gas station who imitated his stutter when he thought he didn't know? Oh no Bill thought as he moved up the stairs to retrieve the quietened device, it was only the start, only the start.

AND IF YOU THINK HIS SUIT ISN'T MADE IN NEW HAMPSHIRE

Arkenay stood in the doorway livid with rage, anger and insult boiling up inside a wellspring of indignation, disgust. It was too much, too far, too great to allow never mind support. Never having felt this way it was all Arkenay could do to hold in check, to stand rather than hurl bodily into Chamais' office. Arkenay knew the depth of feeling was radiating outwards signaling to all and sundry. The entire floor staff had shrunk back and away from Chamais' office, far enough to be unobserved but close enough to hear and feel. Arkenay braced, breathed in, stepped across the threshold and stood.

To any other observer Arkenay's three meter frame was graceful, slight and steadily erect. No outward signs presented, all being nondescript save a small tic in one finger and the slightest dip of one earlobe regularly up and down under the close cropped fur. To Arkenay's kind however this primal display of anger bordered closely on blood lust. Even three millennia of genetics and development could not rid either the outward signs or the hardwired reaction of those seeing it.

Chamais glanced across and noted the lack of deference, Arkenay's omission – quite deliberately – of the required bow and request for entry. It is entirely expected and of my own doing he mused.

"Enter and speak Arkenay."

Arkenay took a step and halted two meters from Chamais' desk, precisely at the limit of personal space.

"I would speak of the project. I would not talk as birthmates. I would not talk as partners. I will talk as one inside to one outside. I would express my disquiet at the path taken. I come to correct the error of your ways."

Chamais was taken aback at first by the strength, but then by the formality of the language used. It followed the ancient pattern of challenge, the call to the fight. Chamais stood, dismissing the desk. With a mental switch the walls and door space became opaque. It would not do for staff to hear or see this bitter exchange, particularly between teacher and student. My first words will be to reconcile.

"I would hear you, and as birthmates talk. In what wise have I given offense?"

Arkenay straightened. "The planet. The policy. The placements that have taken decades you would throw away by bringing them to light. You ask of offense, is not the destruction of sixty years work on a whim cause enough?"

"Whim?" Chamais allowed a show of strength, a slight flicker across one eyelid. Arkenay was brilliant, some said perhaps a genius. Chamais had allowed both freedom and camaraderie to Arkenay and the section that some called heretical and others wanton folly. Over the years this policy produced results, but this tirade could not be sanctioned.

Chamais spoke slowly, measuring the carefully aimed insult.

"You speak unknowingly. You speak as both child and apostate. You speak as our forebears, as one not yet standing upright. You lack wisdom. You lack subtlety. Why should I grant you air?"

Arkenay reeled. Although rage was unabated, Chamais' riposte had torn through the armor. My words will not be heard, my voice lost, my height lowered Arkenay realized. The tic stopped, the earlobe steadied. Arkenay placed hands on mouth, bowed until chin touched chest, waiting. Chastened but not dissuaded.

Chamais allowed a pause. "My birthmate has replaced the

bridge. We will speak. You think it wrong what has been done?"

Arkenay raised his head. "I do not understand. We wait in silence and dark, and we are to now shine the light on them? Always we are reminded to stay in the shadow."

"As we have. Yet they are now both us and they. The shadows were for the first, the light for the followers. Have you thought how the plan could be fulfilled any other way?"

"We have done the same on countless other worlds, from shadows safe, and they believed as they must it was of their own doing. But this we change here? We cast off what has worked for what, for risk of detection?"

"There is not the rest, this you know. They differ from all others we have met, this too you know. So why can you think our plan too must not differ?"

Arkenay paused, reflecting. Why? Why. Because the plans, the others, had been Arkenay's shared design, had worked, had brought Arkenay's height up. In this change Arkenay had not been consulted, had been ignored; taken as insult. Arkenay's anger dispersed. Pride had touched, had burned. Was not this the curse of the race? They had moved beyond, yet once more Arkenay was reminded of the fault line possessed.

Chamais saw the change immediately. "You understand in part?"

Arkenay nodded silently.

"Then would I bring you wisdom. Would you receive?"

"Yes." Again with head low.

"Then hear and we will grow." A small gesture brought chairs as the floor molded itself up to fit them, the room seemingly dissolving as they floated in a field of stars.

"That which you designed for other places could not work here, so you were not joined for this effort. Once we knew them we knew it could not. Why should we take you from success in hundreds and condemn you to failure in one? You were not consulted after the first report."

"It is true. What I have learned I have learned elsewise."

"And therein your fault. You do not understand them."

The black star spattered space filled with a blue green globe, a faintly glowing jewel.

"All of the species on the worlds met to this one had come, as we did, to the point of communal action. Thinking of the common good, none placing themselves too high, with reason and argument defining their paths. This is so?"

"Yes, in all. Leaders chosen by ability, populations not easily troubled and distanced from savagery."

"Open to ideas, open to the force of argument and fact, open to us. So in that manner we came to them, in quiet and in dark, unknown and unobserved, free to influence and to mold and place, letting fact and idea seep through unseen. To go, to change, to return. And to those we have visited?"

"As if they themselves had thought and directed, as it must be. No one individual, no one group shown as catalyst. The only way to take root. And it has worked, for hundreds we have guided to safety and they do not yet see our hand and never will."

"There is truth. They must believe it is their own to hold. As these must." Chamais nodding to the globe.

"But this cannot be. You would have us stand to the front, to be seen, to be heard, to lead. How? They will see, they will know. At best they will be lost, at worst destroyed. It is to this I fear."

Chamais regarded Arkenay kindly. "This is where you fail. These do not look to the group, but to the individual. They disregard reason on the basis of emotion. They do not consider the next ten years, much less the next hundred. They are as we were and how we could be if we so chose. But we do not. They do. And for us to remain in the shadows would achieve nothing. Do you think this has no foundation?"

"No, it must be as you say. You do not speak without reason."

"And you think no plan lies beneath?"

"I do not know if one does or does not."

"So may your wisdom grow. Their very hysteria was nearly our undoing. When we first discovered them and knew we must act they thought the skies were full of us, from many places. They became more and more obsessed and vigilant. Every light, every meteor indeed the stars and planets themselves and even their own transportation was believed us, belligerent, scheming. In fifteen of their years we went twice, yet to us was attributed thousands. Unlike your plans ours had to place us unsupported and modified into their midst. Permanently."

"Modified? Permanently?"

"As male and female they are, we had to be and so we were modified. They live for but one fifth our span, so we must be as they. We cut our lives to match. This is the greater sacrifice. Consider one, alone, changed, life foreshortened. For the good of an unreasoning whole. We could not stay unnoticed, and would not remain undiscovered." Chamais rotated the globe and pointed to a patch of light brown in blue.

"So here and here we placed into areas of strife, dissent and danger, chances of our hand being seen minimized. Places having no form of regular rule, no identification, no law except that of survival. Only here could we enter. Then, as conditions fell, as other areas opened to help, we joined the flow from danger to safety. We arrived welcomed and unquestioned, given legitimacy and place. Which itself was not enough."

Chamais shifted slightly. "We learned their hysteria and fears are easily roused and with difficulty assuaged. Even as respected individuals in their new areas we were met with hostility or anger if we rose, spoke, or chose to be apart from the group. Yet they only look to those apart for leadership. They gave peace on one turn and hatred the next, and cited the same reasoning for both."

Arkenay was stunned. This was beyond knowledge. "How can this be? Is this a place of lost minds? It cannot be, their technology points to high intelligence, but that? Yet if you say it has been observed — "

"As it has and as it is. So the plan was built to change, to break how we have worked before and yes, even go against all. If we do not they are lost. If we do they may be lost. Do you see the reasoning? Do you understand the risk?"

"I see, I am made wise. I see your greater knowledge. I do not see the solution."

"It is before us, within their hysteria, prejudice and hate. One who comes from elsewhere out of mercy may not rise, but one born to someone who came from mercy may. They are accepted as their own, as proof of their moral and societal supremacy. So Arkenay, you say you are made wiser. Given this, if this were your plan, what is it that you would do?"

Arkenay paused. To build on ignorance and emotion over reason to save? "We must rise to the light, but not we ourselves but our children. They will not accept us; they will not accept our voice in the dark. If so our voice must be in the light."

"Correct my birthmate. Do you see both error and wisdom?"

Arkenay nodded. "Yes, I do."

Chamais motioned open the door. "Water has passed. It is as it was. Leave in wisdom."

Arkenay left, disturbed but settled. Chamais let the door seal, remaining seated facing the globe, remembering. It had taken eighty years of patience, placing fifty in the lower hemisphere. Placed deliberately in danger, poverty and disease. Barely two thirds had managed to cross to the more civilized parts of the globe as refugees, obtaining shelter, safety and ultimately legitimacy. Of those a chosen dozen had managed to cross to the final destination, the large northern continent. Those left behind became industrial and financial leaders, bringing wealth and power to support. The children bred true and although fully of there were yet fully of here.

Which held of those who went to the final place. These too had children, built bases of industry, wealth and knowledge. In truth it was all too simple, once nearly in error, far too advanced. Built and now applied as the plan came to climax. Control and power, to save them from something they did not even conceive. And for this the children were the key, accepted as their own.

They would be surprised if they knew the truth of five of the eight presented to their people. Their entertainment, paranoia, imagination and fears would fall far short of what those five held.

All had worked tirelessly, selflessly, continually. This all the more poignant as they knew they were abandoned to live, work and die on and for an alien world that would pay them no heed. Even more for their children, knowing heirs of a civilization they would never see.

That their work was invaluable was not in dispute. The greatest heights of altruism at times requires the basest depravities. And to Chamais, Arkenay and all their kind a life of seeking profit and power to the exclusion of all else by any means was abhorrent, the very antithesis of their culture, their beliefs. But as those on the planet would say, needs must.

After all Presidential campaigns don't come cheap.

YESTERDAY AND TOMORROW ARE TODAY

I had a strange and wonderful relationship with my girlfriend. She had precognition myopia, the only person who will have it she said. She couldn't remember the past, only the future. She only knew the future the way I remember the past. Vaguely and obtusely, except for those things only a handful of years away.

This suited me fine, perhaps it was the only way I could find love. My past is best forgotten, best lost, but that's not the human condition. Except for her. She couldn't really relate to anyone who lives their life in the past, cherishing and reliving memories. To her it was emptiness and void. So I suited her too I guess, my past hidden, my only desire to look forward.

For her, school was terrifying. She went in clearly knowing everything to be gained in the six grades above her, together with vague understanding of a lifetime's accumulated knowledge to come. No school would take her in the end, too scared and not knowing what to do with one supposedly so precocious.

She grew up emotionally hyper-sensitive, people's emotions and futures molding and twisting her psyche. Imagine having a seven year old's brain and body yet knowing all that goes on in and around a thirteen year old's life, going through puberty and all the associated pains and conflict. Worse, imagine having six years to dwell on it, six years to see it coming, six years to fester and roil inside until the inevitable. Then, to add insult to injury, when it occurs it then ceases to exist. Utterly. Completely.

Five years she mourned before her father's death, tearing her mother's heart out. And when finally he died he passed totally out of existence for her. It was as if he was a mere zephyr, or had never been. To her he truly had not.

I came home late from work last night. She had hanged herself in the garage. She left a note, all it said was 'Why will you cheat on me?'

BUSKER

It's the Silurian's fault Janex thought setting up her gear, if only I'd ignored him. 'It's easy,' he said 'nothing to it, candy from a baby.' Oh yeah. 'Make a mint.' he said so I jumped off here at Carson's World and what do I find? The hardest damned crowd, intellectual, rational, boring as batshit. Not that they aren't friendly, just no heart, all mind. Janex looked at her credset and sighed. And they don't pay, four weeks and still short of my ticket off this rock. Dammit she thought, I should be somewhere else raking it in.

She tapped her throat mic and guitar to make sure they were charged, setting the credset on the ground in front of her. A small crowd had gathered, thirty or forty dressed in the same plain, drab, functional garb. At least they're curious she thought, it's a bigger group than usual too. She coughed gently, cementing her audience's attention.

"Ladies and gentlemen, fine citizens of Carson's World, today I present for your education and interest music from worlds gone by, histories decayed, empires fallen!" The crowd stirred gently. That always gets them, I'm living proof they're superior, outlasting, better.

"Today I bring you music from the most fabled, decayed, tragic world of all. Earth! Yes, old Terra, birth place of man!" She held the n as long as possible, a long, menacing trail setting the audience's antennae vibrating in anticipation. She singled out a juvenile in the front.

"Today I take you back to that place, to the height of their consumerist era as they wantonly squandered their offspring's future to satisfy their own lustful pleasures." Janex drew shocked gasps from the crowd, the juvenile pressing back against the adults with a mix of fear and fascination. "I bring you an anthem, a rallying cry from the heart of that degenerate society as it plunged headlong towards oblivion!"

She hit the first note clear and strong, vocals and guitar subtly augmented. She scanned her audience and saw the first flickers of interest grow, ramping up the sound and starting the characteristic strut. The minutes flashed by and with a flourish on one knee she was finished, letting the last chord linger. One song was enough she knew, just at the limits of their patience and curiosity.

"Thank you, thank you, you're a wonderful, intelligent audience. If you found my small gift interesting please return the favor." motioning to the credset.

This time, instead of the odd one or two ponying up, most of the crowd flashed one forearm or another over the credset. After an animated discussion the adults touched the juvenile's forearm. It scuttled over to the credset, chattered unintelligibly at Janex, and ran off after them.

Janex looked down and smiled. Finally enough, the price of a ticket out of this dump, maybe enough over for some food too. She started packing.

"Did we not say we understand the alien but it does not understand us?" Dontrax asked the child as they walked away from the strange musical human.

"You cannot speak BasEng and it cannot speak Mazkad." Thrmyn, the other parent, continued.

"But I did try." their child replied, one arm wrapped around Thrmyn's leg and the other two mimicking Janex's guitar work, happy to have seen such a strange creature.

Dontrax looked at Thrmyn. "Much of their 'music' I have heard, but this one never. It fills a gap. It was worth the creds to just hear such a contradiction."

Thrmyn shifted half its gaze to Dontrax on the right, and half to the child behind it. "Conflicted and illogical, as is all its kind."

"Unable to understand that what it wants it has. Thankfully all that is left are the wanderers, the story tellers."

"How did it go again?" the child piped. "Can you repeat it?"

Thrmyn cleared its triple windpipes and started up, sounding much like a piccolo bagpipe. It rendered the tune and lyrics as best it could, millennia after the composer and its planet had turned to ash. Surprisingly Thrmyn found itself taken with the tune.

They continued their walk home through the indigo blue city, shadows growing long as the bloated red sun bathed the landscape in russet tones. The ancient tune from the long dead composer wafted gently after them.

"I still fail to see why," Dontrax muttered lost in thought and falling behind "if it's goal was to get no satisfaction, it could not see that the act of trying to obtain satisfaction ensured that it was unable to secure a lack of satisfaction. What a strange, strange species."

THE MACHINE IN THE GHOST

"Oh not again!" Peter looked around the music room. Once neatly stacked sheet music was haphazardly arranged, guitar cases open, the amp on and practice headphones plugged in. Stooping he picked up his Strat, plugged it into the amp confirming the tuning had been shifted down a half tone. Peter put the guitar back and sat down heavily.

Marg stood in the doorway. "You're sure?"

"Yes, no doubt at all. Five weeks, five times always the same." Peter looked up at the clock. "And again it's 2:00 am Saturday."

"Nothing's gone?"

"Not a thing. Just shifted, rearranged."

"Did you hear anything this time?"

"No. Don't even know why I got up, no alarms."

Marg moved closer, putting her hand on his shoulder. "Well I guess we know now, something weird's going on."

"We're going to have to get help."

"From who?"

"I know someone, I'll see them next week. Let's get back to bed. It's finished now as usual." with which they went back across the hall, closing the bedroom door behind them.

In the darkened room the guitar case opened, the Strat rising to knee height. A soft cloth followed, slowly polishing down the fret board and back again. The Strat hovered, spun twice on its long axis, and then gently descended back into the case.

"Polts man, you got polts!" Kent exclaimed from behind John Lennon glasses. "You lucky bugger!"

Peter resisted the urge to toss his coffee into Kent's beaming pock-marked face. He knew why he'd sought Kent out, half knowing the answer but needing confirmation. Well, he'd got it. "Don't know about lucky, but I thought as much about the ghost — "

"Not ghost, poltergeist. You've not seen it? It doesn't play with you, just your gear, only that room?"

Peter shook his head. "Just there, nowhere else, nothing else."

"For sure it's a polt. You planning to keep it?"

Peter glared back. "No, why do you think I called you? Maybe help me tweet at #freakedfromfenderfondlingfantom? No, I want it gone!" He leaned closer to Kent's smoke-stale breath. "It's cluttering my life, freaking me out and nothing, and I mean nothing, is going on Saturday nights because of it, kapische?"

Kent grinned idiotically. "Ok, ok, explains the aggression, I'm hearing you. You've come to the right guy. No dramas, I can fix it." Kent leaned back sucking loudly on his soy latté. "I can do it this Saturday. No charge, it's a service man, a community service. Just one condition."

"Which is?" Peter asked suspiciously.

Kent polished off the latté and leaned forward, leering almost lustfully. "The polt. If I catch it, I keep it. It's mine!"

Eleven o'clock Saturday Kent turned up on Peter's doorstop, Marg deciding to spend the night with her sister. Kent smiled broadly as Peter opened the front door. "Hey man, we're here," waving his free hand behind him "me and my posse!"

Kent brushed past Peter, followed by his two assistants, each carrying a large sports bag. "Meet Barb and Donna, my team."

Each girl turned, smiled, nodded and then headed off down the hall.

"Pleased to meet you I'm sure." Peter called to their backs. Turning to Kent he continued "So what's the plan and what's with the bags?"

"Well it's simple, we've got the traps in the bag and all we do is put them out and wait. C'mon, let's get to it." with which he followed the two girls to the music room.

"Hey nice digs, very nice room my man, just love the wall hangings," Kent crooned walking over and drumming his fingers on a psychedelically painted ukulele hanging over an easy chair "very last century."

"I'm glad you like it but it's show time isn't it?" Peter queried, stepping carefully between the girls and a tangle of wiring, power boards and meters.

"Show time, hmm. Hey Barb tell Pete the drill." looking towards the girl on his left.

"Love to." replied the girl on his right. Kent gave a sheepish grin and shifted his attention to emptying his bag haphazardly on the floor.

"I'll save the technical details but the main thing is that your poltergeist is composed of pure energy."

"Pure electrical energy." chimed Donna.

"Yes, pure electrical energy, so it can be quite easily captured by sending the right voltage through a mesh trap at exactly the right time." Barb reached into her sports bag and pulled out a tightly woven wire mesh cloth.

"We spread it like this," shooing the three of them back to the doorway and placing the sheet in the middle of the room "attach our cabling, trip switches and timers, then get the whole thing live and wait. It doesn't even have to touch down on the sheet, just be, oh, maybe two or three meters away and bingo!"

"Bingo!" exclaimed Kent.

"Bingo?" Peter asked.

"Bingo!" Barb continued, holding up a small gunmetal grey box. "Polt in a box!"

"And no damage, it's all safe?" Peter asked.

"No damage." Donna smiled.

"All safe." Barb chirped.

"That's what the manual says." Kent piped.

Peter spun round. "Manual? What do you mean manual? You've never done this before?"

"Er, um, no, not with this exact method." Kent mumbled.

"Not any other methods." Donna smiled.

"We're actually ghost busting virgins." Barb chirped.

"You're our first." Donna giggled.

"But I've watched the YouTube vid and it looks easy, really." Kent slinked towards the doorway.

Peter just sighed. Too late now, too bloody late. He looked resignedly at Kent. "It looked easy? Really?"

"Absolutely!" Kent grabbed Peter by the shoulders, guiding him out of the room towards the lounge. "Better clear out, let the girls finish. Anyway," he continued half way down the hall "you've got full home insurance?"

With five minutes to go Peter, Barb and Donna were sitting in the lounge watching a small meter box on the coffee table. A thick cable ran from the back of the box down the hall to the mesh sheet. Apart from the solitary lamp in the lounge the house was in darkness.

Kent stood opposite the three of them, his attention caught by Peter's large collection of late-last-century early-this-century records. Kent would stop periodically, give a small girlish squeal of delight and pull one out. Tipping the record out of the sleeve he'd fondle it like an ancient artefact, badly hum what he thought were a few key bars, and hastily return record to sleeve to shelf. Each time Peter winced at the spectacle.

'C'mon Kent," he urged "get over here and tell me what happens now. It's nearly time."

"Ok, ok, just a sec." with which an original copy of Sgt Peppers nearly slipped from his grip. "Yeah, yeah, she loves me." he mumbled, placing the album back. He plodded over and plonked himself down.

"We wait, watch, and" pointing to the meter box "once

the needle hits one hundred we know your polt's there, two hundred it's in range and the autos trip in, then bingo!"

"Bingo." Barb echoed.

"Bingo!" Donna exclaimed.

"Bingo, the power hits, the field collapses and we've got polt in a box! Then this lights up," touching a small red globe on the top of the box "and it's all sealed and safe. I've got a polt, the house goes back to boring normality, and Peter gets to play mummies and daddies on Saturday night."

Barb and Donna tittered as Peter just sat stock still. A few more minutes, just a few and it will be over; electrocution, plot in a box, or total failure.

"Show time kiddies." Kent whispered, leaning forwards expectantly. Hardly had he done so than the needle flickered, wobbled, then jumped to one hundred.

"It's here." Peter breathed.

"Strong, very strong," Donna muttered, pulling Kent's hand from her upper arm "shouldn't be long."

Barb squealed as Kent's hand nearly crushed hers in his tightening grip. "Two hundred! Two hundred! Now, now!" she called, trying to lean forward as Kent tried to pull both girls closer. Peter just watched wide-eyed, more interested than scared.

"Whoa! Three hundred! Five hundred!! It's still climbing!" The needle rushed headlong across the dial face, bending as it tried to smash its way off the gauge. The box smoked gently and then expired in a shower of sparks. As the sickly smell of ozone wafted up, across the room the shelves started to vibrate, records jostling back and forth.

Then the noise hit. Peter fancied that he could see the shock wave hammering down the hallway, screaming, demanding to be heard as it burst into the lounge room. It was a guitar, one perfectly hit and sustained chord, a deafening crescendo that shoved him back in the recliner. The records were torn off the wall and flew straight at Kent who shoved Barb and Donna forward while trying to disappear between the sofa cushions.

The note changed, grew louder and more strident, shifted,

slid and rippled up and down the scale in a frenzied riff. The records circled drunkenly in the air around Kent and the girls. Every couple of seconds one would dive straight for Kent's face, come to a screeching halt inches away, briefly hover drunkenly and then re-join the whirling pack as another took it's place. Peter hardly noticed that the divers were all from his metal collection, festooned with ghoulish artwork. He also didn't notice Kent had noticed, to which the newly formed and rapidly growing wet patch across Kent's groin bore witness. All this accompanied by the girl's strident screaming and Kent's crying.

In the middle of the bedlam, mayhem and ear shattering noise Peter sat rigid, transfixed. The sound was perfect, clear, played brilliantly and crisply, no wavering, fumble, or uncertainty. It was a living thing that possessed and invaded him, lifting him upwards until he hung, arms and legs flung back, floating in the middle of the swirling pack of records. He was part of the music, the sound, the screaming demanding deafening thrust, the guitar elevating the hard rock lead to a place of sublime beauty it had no right to touch, never mind hold.

Seemingly as quickly as it had started it was over. Peter was placed firmly but gently back, the records flew at breakneck speed each to its original place, and the darkened house burst into brightness as all the lights came on. As the last note faded into silence Kent and the girls vaulted over the smoking box, out the door and into Kent's car, leaving in a cloud of tire smoke, screams and urine scented fear.

Peter just sat, drained. He'd never felt playing like that, it was impossible, just impossible. But there it was and (he admitted guiltily) he wanted more. Funny, he was supposed to be getting rid of a malevolent spirit but he wanted to be a part of the music, for it to never stop. He sighed. It still didn't change the fact that something needed to be done.

Peter told Marg the full story the next day, in a house that showed absolutely no signs of anything having happened. Their neighbors also swore that Saturday night had been the quietest night in the street for years.

Marg walked out of the undisturbed house in the quiet street five minutes after Peter had finished.

"Hot shredder or not I am not sharing my house with that," she explained through the driver's side window "you get it sorted, call me at my sister's and I'll be back." With which she sped off, leaving a second burnout mark on the driveway.

Towards the end of the following week Peter realized he still didn't know what he was actually going to do. He'd only seen Kent once, briefly, and that from a distance as Kent ran away. He was left by himself to deal with the problem. It had chosen to scare the daylights out of Kent and the girls but not me – Peter thought – so maybe, just maybe I can reason with it. Maybe I'll just try talking to it.

He slept soundly Friday night, having a plan, no matter how vague, seemingly a help. By 1:59 am Saturday he was sitting relaxed in a chair in the corner of the music room, feeling more comfortable having walls rather than empty space behind him. A final check of his watch, he flipped the floor lamp off with his foot, plunging the music room into darkness.

He counted silently to sixty, shifted slightly, coughed.

"Ah, hello?"

He was answered by silence. Nothing.

"Er, hello?" Just a little louder. Still nothing.

"Hello??" This time it was a bit too loud, startling him. Peter realized he was getting nervous. He tried again, in what he hoped was a friendly tone.

"Hello? Are you there? I'd like to talk." Still nothing, but his left foot felt cold. Could that be it?

"Is that you? Are you here?" Still silence, but now both of his feet and calves were cold. Ok, it's here but not talking. Could it be upset over last week?

"Look, I'm sorry about last week's effort, it's … well …we were both scared you know, but — "

"Your friend's a twat!" The voice was soft, measured,

English with a touch of peevishness. To Peter's horror it came from just behind his left ear. It was all he could do not to run away screaming in terror; as it was he'd taken a death grip on the arms of the chair and was shaking.

"Your apology is accepted," the voice now behind his right ear "but I'd have thought you had better tastes in friends yeah?" the voice now in front of him.

"Well, oh I'm, it's just, he's sorta … " Peter stammered out, still quivering.

"C'mon you can't be that scared, I mean you came in here, waited and want to chat. I'm glad you didn't bring wotzitz with you, he's a complete tosser."

"Maybe, but I didn't know anyone else who knew anything about gh … I mean, well, the undea … I mean … "

"Wot, you mean things that go twang in the night?" The voice laughed. "Yeah, your mate's really smart, lotsa help. He ran every red light for miles and spent the next two nights cowering in a church."

"He won't even talk to me now. Maybe it was stupid but what else was I going to do? I don't know the first thing about this. So it was a mistake — "

"But you've wised up?"

"I have, so I'm here now." Peter found himself relaxing and leant back, his foot moving unconsciously towards the floor lamp switch.

"Wouldn't do that if I were you laddie."

"Huh?" Peter froze.

"The switch. Light. You know I'm not really all here yeah, just enough to do the job, I'm not built proper if you know what I mean."

Peter cautiously moved his foot away from the switch. "Sorry, didn't realize."

"S'ok. So I'm here, you're here, what's eating you?"

"I thought it was obvious. You turn up once a week, play my guitar and stuff — "

"I put it all back, I'm careful — "

"But we know you've been here, we've got no idea about you. I mean, one minute it's the Strat, what's next? Knife wielding puppets? Chainsaws? I've never met a dead person before."

"I didn't want to be dead — "

"I didn't mean that — "

"… and I didn't want to hang around down here," the voice continued in a melancholy tone "it's not like I planned this."

"I didn't say you had, I just … "

"You know it's not normal yeah?"

"What, talking to the dead? Thought everyone did it."

"Smartarse! You want I should go?"

"Yes, I mean, no, look, it's just a bit … different … talking to you."

"Well I haven't had company for a while so s'cuse me manners ok? Do you want to know how I got like this? You know it's rare yeah? Ever wondered why you aren't all knee deep in the dear departed?"

"To be honest no, it's never crossed my mind. But I guess there are a lot of dead people."

"A few million year's worth. And hardly any are here. It's rare. So listen. Do you remember when that big scientific tunnel in Europe, you know, that tube thingy … "

"CERN?"

"Yeah, that's him, CERN. Yeah, do you remember when they found that big hose on wotzitz particle … "

"The Higgs boson?"

"Yeah, that's it, that thing. Remember that?"

"No, I wasn't born then but I read about it in school and Marg — "

"Anyway, so I'm driving near that thing with a blonde piece and she's getting busy you know — "

"No, I don't know — "

"Well you should find out — "

"That's why I'm trying to sort this out."

"So," the voice continued with emphasis "I get badly distracted – or goodly you could say – and next thing I know we're off the road hurtling across a paddock and then straight into a tree and I'm dead, but at the same time they made that higgs wotzitz, exactly the same time, and that's why I'm here and not gone."

"Because of the Higgs boson?"

"Yeah, I read a bit about it later and I must have gotten tangled up with a — "

"Hold on! You're him? That was, I mean only one — "

"Yeah yeah, me, now you know. Guess you've read about me?"

"Of course, I've got all your albums and all that and it explains the music last week. Holy … you're in my house?! Wow!!"

"Hey, don't go all stupid on me, I'm dead remember."

"Yeah but you're still you, I mean, this is crazy — "

"Ok, fine, I'm here, it's me, but just don't expect Hendrix or Clapton to come floating down and do a set with me yeah? It's just me and as far as I know maybe thirty others around and they don't play."

"Well compared to you who did? Seriously, who ever could? I bet they like listening to you, you know, free gigs and all."

"Ha!" The voice was derisive. "You got no idea. Do you know what I did all day, all night? Watch. It's all I could do. Couldn't sleep, materialize, grab stuff or nuthin', not a damned thing. Except."

"Except?"

"Except here. Near you. I don't know why."

"You must."

"Why? I'm not blinking Einstein am I? I'm a, I mean I used to be a guitarist so how do I know? I left school in third grade and you want me to know how this works? Leave it out!"

"But why me? Why here? It's so out of the way, you expect me to believe you just floated in?"

"Do you have any idea how boring it is being dead? Do you? It was fun for a bit man, you know, after I'd just gone, reading my obits and watching it all fold out. But after that? Zip. Nada. Bugger all."

"I'd never — "

"I know, I'm not being narky, just sayin'. It was so boring, so bleedin' Swiss boring, god those people! So straight, dull, grey. It got too much, I had to escape, so I started walking and didn't stop until I got here."

The voice paused, then continued slowly.

"Six weeks ago, do you remember your loo jamming up?"

"Of course, cost me two hundred dollars for the plumber."

"Sorry, that was me."

"You? Why'd you block my toilet?"

"I didn't mean to," the voice continued defensively "I'd just come walking along, minding my own business and then bang! I materialize in the middle of your sewer pipe. I didn't know what was going on, I'd never materialized before."

"It wasn't a disaster, I mean just a bit of backflow upstairs, it could've been worse."

"For you yeah, but me? I'm just wandering along and it's my face passing through the s-bend and it hits what you've deposited and I materialize, stuck there, I can't move, you're still going about your business … "

Peter nearly held back his first peal of laughter.

"Oh yeah, it's ok for you to laugh innit, but guess what? I materialized just high enough to put me eyes, nose and mouth in the right place facing upstream and working perfectly for the first time since I'm dead and what do I get? Your processed vindaloo!"

"Oh hell, I'm sorry," lurching out between gasps "you poor oh jeez — "

"Hey, it took me two flippin' hours to work out how to dematerialize and your plumber was sending it all down with a plunger! And the Rota-Rooter?!?! Hell, have you any idea … " with which the voice choked, spluttered, and then dissolved into laughter.

"Alright, alright," the voice continued after it had recovered "yeah I guess it's bleedin' hilarious and all that but the point is it was an accident, until I hit here I couldn't do nuthin' to the physical world, couldn't pick up anything or that or anything. And I miss it, you know, so bad I miss it, just to sit and jam and blow out the cobwebs."

Peter looked over to where he thought his guitars lay. "I know what you mean, I'd go spare if I couldn't play …"

"… torture man, total torture."

"I know it's not the same but at least you can listen, I'm not anywhere as good but I'm not too bad — "

The voice coughed loudly. "Look, no offence and all that but as a guitarist you've got nuthin."

"Oh c'mon, it's not that bad."

"It is, I mean, technically you're ok but you're too rigid, too tight, too much the notes. I mean, look around here, you got all those music sheets yeah?"

"So?"

"You know I never had a one? Phil neither and he wrote all our stuff. You've got to feel your way around, live it. Without that you're like everyone else, cold, flat, no mojo. It's gotta flow."

"Nah! I feel it — "

"But only when you sing, your voice's cool but your playin's stiff, drags it down. It don't jump across and maybe it never will. That's the only difference, you and me, stiff and flow."

"You're kidding me? Surely, I mean you've — "

"No, honest mate, I'm not. Technically speaking it's four fingers, six strings and a pick so we're equal, but it's the flow you can't teach. It's either come out, in there waiting to come out, or not there. And I gotta say, sorry you know, but what I heard it aint there."

Peter groaned inwardly. Yeah, it was right. "Ok, I guess you're right. Maybe I'll just give it up."

"No way, it's not cat scratching it's just it don't fly. Your singing is different, but your playin's holding you back."

"Hey, you don't suppose you could help me, I mean teach me? If you could, well, maybe it'd work."

"Nope, told you, you can't teach, you gotta have. Maybe if you felt it that could help, maybe. The only chance you'd have would be if you could be me or … " the voice trailed off into silence.

Peter sat wondering. "You don't suppose you could?"

"If you mean what I think you mean then maybe, I think, maybe, but you as a puppet?"

"Could it be just a bit? I mean, just the arms, just the guitar. Could you? Could I control … "

"I think, I mean, yeah, should be ok. It's your body, I'd be a guest, you could kick me out."

"Just once maybe? Let me feel it once, for myself, to know?"

"Yeah, ok, yeah it should be ok, just once. Which one you want to use?"

"The Strat."

"Sweet, damned sweet." A hard wooden form brushed against Peter's knee. "There she is, plugged in and live. You ready?"

Peter cradled the guitar carefully. "Yeah, I guess." Deep breath, relax, stop shaking. "What do I do?"

"Relax yeah, I'm not sure." the voice replied. "I've got an idea, it sorta worked last week with your cat so I guess, but if it gets too weird just say something, boot me out yeah?"

"Sorta? Well, ah, ok."

"Ok, here we go."

The room grew quiet for a minute or two. Peter felt a small patch of cold and damp on his forehead that slowly sank from outside to inside.

– Just like an ice-cream headache. Peter thought.

– God I could go a magnum now. the voice in Peter's head commented.

Peter blanched. – Hell, you're in here!

– Yeah, you knew this'd be it. Gotta say there's lotsa interesting shit going on in here.

– Oh you're not —

– Nah, just joking. I'm behaving. It feels good, to have fingers, to touch, ones I don't have to generate. You're just like the cat, I'm workin' out where the pedals are. How you doin'?'

– Not bad, a bit weird but. What now?

– Well, your body, your choice. Make it a good one yeah.

Ideas?

Peter laughed. – You know if there's only one shot there's only one choice.

– Thunder and lightning?

It took the first few bars but Peter managed to forget his guitar, forgot that someone else was controlling his fingers flying up and down the fretboard, and just let it happen. It had never been like this for him, the guitar so effortless, sweet. He flung his head back, dropped out all inhibition and fear, and let loose.

Five minutes later Peter sat eyes blazing, pumped up on the edge of the chair as the last notes bounced back across the room at him.

– Holy mother of … flipping heck.

– You see it now? Do you feel it? How good can you be when you let go! Your voice, my fingers —

– More, c'mon, let's go again!

– Which one?

– Who cares, anything!

And off they went without hesitation or respite, a mad musical orgy of reckless abandon. For hours they continued, Peter's arms burning with fire, finger tips screaming and near bloodied, his voice growing hoarse as the sweat cascaded down across his guitar and chair. Peter prayed it would never stop, that it could never stop; but the dim light of a late autumn's dawn crept teasing through the curtains, bringing them to a halt.

After so many hours the silence was deafening, torpid.

– Thanks, that was worth the wait yeah. The voice was soft in his head.

– That was unbelievable! I'm the one that should be thanking you.

– It's no biggie, just a shame that's gonna be it.

– Huh?

– You know, Marg? Why you talked to me in the first place? No more spook yeah? It's respect innit, you're not a bad bloke, I don't want to be a weight you know.

A surge of panic hit Peter. – No! I mean, I don't want you

to go, I don't want to never have that again.

– You wouldn't mind if I hung around? If I played through you?

– If we could keep it from her …

– … well I'm not gonna tell …

– … and I won't …

– … so it's guess a deal yeah …

– Yes, a deal. I'll tell her I scared you off …

– … I'll pull my head in and leave your stuff alone …

– … until we pull out the guitars. But how'll I find you?

– Just think, I'll leave a bit of me in here, you just call.

– Call what?

– I've got a name. the voice laughed.

Peter paused, looking up to the ceiling now bathed in the light of a new day. He continued out loud.

"You know, I've always dreamed of being in a band, a good band."

– Most have, it's way common.

"I didn't think I was good enough …" Peter trailed off into silence.

– But? the voice cajoling, teasing.

"Well, I don't suppose you'd consider hitting the road again?"

– Baby, the voice crooned – baby I thought you'd never ask.

TRANSITION

Atop the rise the Southern Lord cast his gaze to the camp of the Lord of All Lands. He fancied he could see him smiling, self-satisfied. As well he should be as this, the fifth day of battle, belonged to him. The featureless plain between them, barely a half hours ride across, formed the narrow waist of all the known lands. To either side lay the harsh oceans with their monsters and devils; to the North the lands of his opponent, rich, fertile and warm; and to the South his cold, harsh and unforgiving home, once part of the Lord of All Lands kingdom until he had wrested it away. It seemed fitting that this place should decide two fates, bringing all the world again under one hand. God willing it would be his.

He shifted slightly, his mount gently snorting at the change. God willing indeed, if God was still willing. The smoke from funeral pyres rose lazily as both sides tended their fallen, piles of swords and sandals growing as the dead were relieved for the living's needs. With the day's battle over and the counting yet to be done he knew that for the fourth time he had been bested, and although not broken it was becoming more a question of when than if. Only the setting sun betrayed hope, its blue rays seemingly painting his standard on the clouds. A small portent, not grand or clear, but a portent none the less. He hung his head in silent prayer, dedicating the day to God in His glory, himself to His service, and begging for the doubt to go.

A gentle cough interrupted his thoughts. "m'Lord seems troubled."

He looked down at his priest, a wizened old man of forty winters, and sighed. Had his brother not said he resembled this one's visage? Indeed, the cares of campaigning weighed heavy.

"The day has been lost, as have those before." He looked around to see no one else within earshot. "I have asked again if my cause be just, if God be for me. Again, I have no reply."

The priest frowned, pulling back the shroud from his cassock. "To doubt is our lot m'Lord, but our cause is without doubt. Do you question the vision?"

"No, and it returns atimes."

"And should we not stand closer, should one not be oppressed by the other unjustly? Have you not been chosen by God to remove the yoke of the northerner from all our necks? These things you know, these things the very voice of God gave to you m'Lord, and you doubt?"

He leant down in earnest, pained speech. "Yes, all things are as you say, in my bedchamber in solitude do they come, yet in the light of day I am abandoned." He straightened, pointing out across the plain. "I see not the hand of God in mine but with the oppressor. It is not his fellows that outnumber in death but mine. My arrows do not fly true, my sword is not sharpened but theirs are! Is that the hand of God upon my shoulder?" He leant back towards the priest. "Why is this?"

The priest smiled. "God tests those that are chosen, and as the testing so the choosing. It is clear that tested you are, and the greatness of the cause lies hand in hand. Is it for nothing the metal is heated, hammered and chilled? Does a sword arise gently from the field? No m'Lord, no and again no, and as they so you. The hand of God lies heavy upon you, and to your enemy's pride shall come desolation. This is the truth of God m'Lord."

He leant down, one hand on the priest's shoulder. "Your counsel is wise, as always. Pray forgive my lack of faith."

"Forgiveness m'Lord is always yours. But you must attend vigil tonight, not only for your sake but for ours. For as your faith so the faith of those who follow."

He wheeled around. "I will keep vigil with you tonight priest, and faith God is with us." With which he cantered off the ridge, back to his encampment, the priest jogging after.

Dismounting on his arrival he was greeted by his master at arms. He bore the marks of the day in the field, a combination of sweat, caked dust and grass, still wet blood splattered across chest and arms.

"m'Lord, m'Grace, God favors us with your safe return." He bowed his head quickly, but not fast enough that his fatigue and doubt went unnoticed.

Tiredness and doubt – the Southern Lord thought – the seeds of defeat. He clasped him firmly on his shoulders. "Ludwig, the favor falls to me. How went the day?"

"Fairly but not to us." Ludwig smiled, noting his Lord's appearance to be worse than his own. For each mark and furrow he bore, his Lord's were double and deeper. "We have new arrivals, more men from the far steppes. If it pleases m'Lord after you have reviewed them your tent is prepared."

"No Ludwig, tonight I keep vigil. So to the review."

"As m'Lord pleases. Is it," with which he became hesitant "again the dreams?"

He remained silent as they walked through the camp. His men, his army, each one a volunteer. Each one had willingly laid family and life aside to follow him, to follow the voice and hand of God as it led him on. And all the time he was pursued by the dreams. Visions of a world with men and women unshackled from a life of being owned and bought to being their own masters under an enlightened and honest ruler. Where what a man was meant more than who a man was. They all knew this of the dreams, but none save the priest knew of the balance. The vision like smoke, generated by the fire of bloodshed and toil, of death and obedience and sacrifice under him. The dreams never wavered, never shifted, the one followed the other, smoke after fire, war before peace, sacrifice before victory, death before life. And between, always between, the symbol rising up, two blue crescent moons touching back to back above the fire to be consumed, then returning and purging the lands. Neither he nor the priest could account for the symbol, what it meant or portended; that lay for God alone.

"Yes Ludwig," as they reached the knot of new soldiers "the dreams."

At their approach the men had fallen into rough lines. The three of them walked slowly in front of the assembly as he spoke of the vision, the reason for the fight, the hope that kept them here. He was nearly finished when he was pulled up short by a person in the third rank.

"Master at arms, that man," he called, pointing "bring him forwards." The assembled men froze as Ludwig moved, appearing shortly with one of their number in tow. The man was hardly that, barely two thirds Ludwig's height, dressed in rags, skin hardened, calloused and cracked. One arm was covered by a leather sleeve, the knife in its scabbard nearly reaching from shoulder to elbow, the pike on his back nearly touching the ground. It was not this that caught the Southern Lord's attention but the hair; the left bore shoulder length braided locks, the right peach fuzz newly grown.

He leant forward to the now bowed head in front of him and folded the right ear forwards. He sighed and lifted the face up gently by the chin. As I thought, a child, a refugee.

Softly but clearly, as if to his own son, he asked "How old are you child?"

"I think I am eleven winters if it pleases m'Lord."

"And from which estate did you escape?"

"The vineyards of Cultharen on the north sea m'Lord."

"You came to fight?"

The eyes lit up. "Yes, my friends remain, unable to flee m'Lord, I would fight to free them."

Eleven. Four winters from manhood. Too far. "You may not fight," and seeing the crestfallen look on the boy's face "you are but a child! There are other ways to fight without the sword."

The child prostrated himself on the ground, but even in that act there was an air of defiance. "m'Lord cannot! I have been sent by God, I have heard Him command me! How could I escape my masters, how could I travel if not God is with me? Already I have baptized my dagger with northerner's blood, I have pledged my life to your service and fight! This you cannot do."

The priest crouched close to the child. "As your Lord commands, so must it be done. You are too young, this is men's work. If you have pledged your life so must you have pledged your obedience."

The child paid him no heed. "No m'Lord, I beg of you. I have been sent to fight, I have been sent to bring you victory, you must permit me!" with which he reached forwards and grasped the Southern Lord's left foot. A shocked gasp was broken only by the sound of Ludwig's sword being drawn. The Southern Lord looked down and blanched, raising his left hand.

"Stay your weapon!" In reaching out the child's sleeve had shifted up revealing his forearm. There, in plain sight, were two blue crescent moons touching back to back atop a pillar of fire. Was this the sign he had asked for? He continued to stare until he became aware that all eyes had shifted to him, expectantly.

"Child, get up. Now look at me. The mark on your arm. Where did you get it?"

"It has always been with me. I cannot remember not having it m'Lord."

"And when did God command you come?"

"Two winters ago, m'Lord, God commanded me to seek the sun rising in the south and to bring victory to His chosen, m'Lord, to you."

"Do you have a name?"

"Eous m'Lord."

"Then Eous, you will fight for me." He motioned to one of his officers. "Gaplan, take Eous with you, he is to fight with your ranks."

When at last the three of them were alone again the priest

turned to him. “m’Lord, the mark was the same as your visions?”

“One and the same priest. He is sent, of this I am sure.” Turning to Ludwig he continued, “See to it that Gaplan does not spare Eous from the fight. Take a care to watch over him and bring me word at the close of the morrow. Now priest, let us to vigil. I believe I shall not sleep this night.”

Three nights hence the Southern Lord sat again on the rise, dusk casting long shadows as his men prepared to commit their dead to the heavens by fire. Today, as the last three, he knew he had bested his opponent and greatly; yet for all it was worth his mood and that of his men was subdued. He saw the Lord of All Lands’ funeral pyres ignite. You have lost five men to each of mine, but oh what men I have lost.

The priest slowly gained the top of the rise, wiping bloodied hands on his cassock. “m’Lord, all is ready.”

Silently they turned down to his men, living surrounding the dead piled carefully on their wooden heaps. That the naked corpses were his he was of no doubt, but recognizing individuals was hard, the work of the enemies’ blades and cudgels being thorough. If it were not for the right gloves laid before each, patterned and inscribed with the clan shield, some may have yet remained unnamed. Save for the small, pale body atop the smallest pyre, arm drooping across his brothers in fallen embrace, the gash to his side evidencing the blade that took his life. Even at this distance the Southern Lord fancied he could see the two crescent moons. Eous.

Had it truly only been three days he was amongst us and such a change wrought? He had watched as Eous first joined in battle, the unconventional, eager, even fanatical way he had driven into his opponents, scything down the best and bravest without pause, seeming unstoppable and unbreakable. How this had drawn his men to the same place, infusing his army with such energy and vigor they wished that the sun would never set, that the day’s work could continue until the enemy was routed. From the Southern Lord his men had learned to believe that their cause was right, that victory should be theirs;

Eous had raised them to a place where no other reality could exist, where their very countenances showed only victory and strength. Until dusk, at the very end of this day's contest, to the one chance blade unseen that cut their champion down.

Smoke curled from the base of the pyre, an oily black snake barely discernible against the darkening indigo sky. A small flicker and a red orange glow licked at its base, seemingly dodging in and out of the kindling in dance macabre. The Southern Lord lowered his gaze.

"Men's hearts are brittle things in war. More is gained or lost in belief than most think. I fear this may be enough."

The priest was silent, measuring thought and word in equal part. His mood was one with the men, one with his Lord. To him the smoke was transporting his hope, maybe even his faith, on zephyred fingers into … what? What fills a void created by the loss of that which had filled another void? A man without a trade is still a man, but a priest robbed of his faith, now what is that? He felt a dampness on his cheek, confirmed by touch a tear. Funny he thought, not since a whelp. He let his hand fall back within his cassock.

"m'Lord, I fear I have built too much on this one child, the sign, my ignorance and lack — "

"No, there is no fault in you or in God." He shifted his gaze back to the pyre, now a ruddy bright orange blotch against the blackness of night. The flames had leapt, claiming their prize, greedily fingering the small frame of Eous. A gush, a roar, and his body disappeared behind a crimson veil.

"Sign he was and sign he remains, living or dead. His leaving can only mean that our course is not in God's plan, our blessing passed. It is at my feet that the blame is laid, why I do not know but it is the same. It was my vision, my calling."

Across the valley the Lord of All Lands' pyres burned bright, outnumbering and outshining his. He knew it did not matter, how many more dead were there than here. In one small body his men's hearts were entombed, to be turned to ash. He laughed, a coarse, hacking, cynical bray to which all ears were drawn.

"It is one thing to win with blood on your hands but to lose is another. My reckoning and judgement to come will be great. We cannot lay our arms down, we cannot undo what we have started. I may not win the day but fight on I must. Yet to carry others to death for a cause I think right — "

The cry of thousands of voices silenced him. A shaft of piercing blue white light fell from the heavens on Eous' pyre, bathing the valley in blue ice. Shaking as were they all, the priest could clearly see the Lord of All Lands and his army caught in the light, riveted solid. Their faces mirrored the fear in him and in his Lord's men. All eyes were locked on that shaft, barely wide enough to encompass the pyre's base, a seemingly unbreakable bond cementing heaven to earth.

The pyre shattered to a golden orb, ascending slowly, gracefully, to tree top height. Glowing ever brighter it stopped, seeming suspended from the shaft of light. The orb shivered, rippled, spread to a disc, a square and then, as the cry caught in the Southern Lord's throat, to a shape, a figure, a man … Eous.

The cry from his men was silenced, all eyes locked on Eous bright golden and smiling, arms outstretched and whole. Bearing no scars of battle, no wound or bruise, no shadow was cast as the light fell through him and out within the Southern Lord's men, across the valley to the Lord of All Lands' camp.

The Southern Lord felt linked to his men as if they were now one body, one being, one mind. He heard – no he felt – the priest transfixed beside him, could sense every fiber of him, of his men, seeing through each and every mans' eyes as he knew they could through his. The quiet in his camp was total, drenching, not even the sound of breath to disturb. Across the valley wailing cries of terror roiled, rolling and battering useless against the walls of his camp.

Eous smiled, voice gentle but strong cutting through the valley, the peace, the noise. To the Southern Lord and his men no words were needed, but rather Eous was within their minds, feather light. The rising wail across the valley spoke of a greeting of fear rather than peace.

"I am of you."

"Eous." the camp whispered.

"Together we have struggled, we have fought. Do you think our cause lost, our path unjust? You are flesh and blood as was I but now, now I am more," with which his light grew, turning night into day "and this too awaits all of you."

"I was sent to bring victory. I was sent to raise your hearts and spirits, I was sent to affirm your cause as righteous, to bring the rising sun from the south to all lands."

The Southern Lord felt drawn up, fuller and stronger, leaning towards Eous with outstretched arms and eager eyes, heart seemingly bursting from his chest, as around him his men were the same, as one.

"I am sent, you are called. Hear me! It is God's will that you lift the northern yoke of oppression from His people, to rend the veil of darkness!" The light, now blinding white, intense, painful, held them still. Eyes wide open, unable and unwilling to move, Eous filled their vision and minds, hearts and souls, his voice now a crashing ocean demanding to be heard, a visceral, tangible force.

"You are chosen for this work. Victory is yours, all you need do is grasp it, take it! Remove doubt from your hearts, God is always with you, his hand upon you and his spirit guiding!"

Eous started to rise again, arms outstretched facing them as he climbed higher. "Behold I go to join our brothers, to prepare your place, to stand! And I leave you with a sign, a remembrance of me for all to see!"

All eyes followed Eous up until all that could be seen was a spot, a dot where the light ended. A blazing flash horizon to horizon, accompanied by a thunderclap, and Eous was gone. Across the valley could be heard the sounds of men screaming, weapons thrown aside as they fled in headlong panic away from the Lord of All Lands, away from the Southern Lord, away from the spectre of certain defeat.

Around him the Southern Lords men's eyes burned blue grey, as did his, the lasting mark of the chosen of heaven. Weapons held aloft, faces bright burning, they turned to him.

He unsheathed his sword, and, as one, they ran forward to claim the victory now theirs.

A polite but warm round of applause broke around the cruiser *Aristarchus'* operations room. The last flickers of the high-altitude detonation had faded, the planet below returning to night. Commander Shelby leant forward, removing her skull cap.

"Well done. Textbook execution and delivery. Stand down watch, relief until tomorrow's de-brief. It's all yours OpsCon."

Stepping down from her dais with a nod to her second in command, she walked aft to her cabin. Her first full Transition in command, a tough brief but, in the end, it had come off well. A glow of satisfaction rippled through her. Although part of prior Transition teams to actually lead one from end to end was something else. Four years work, time, commitment and sacrifice of her crew to a project that wouldn't – in the ultimate – see a result for a thousand years? Well, it was a different level, a different plane of existence.

A gentle cough behind her dragged her out of her reverie. Turning she saw the slight form of Specialist Ceruto, not yet twenty-five and on her first tour. Reminds me of myself she thought, not for the first time, thirty years ago.

"Yes Ceruto?"

"A minute of the Commander's time ma'am?"

"Of course," motioning Ceruto inside "come in and take a seat." Not that it was a tough choice in Shelby's spartan quarters. A desk with screen, bed and two chairs were supplemented by one open wardrobe and a tiny, ostentatious collection of books.

She knew what Ceruto was going to ask. In fact, she expected to have the same conversation with all fifty of her first tour personnel. She had had the same one with her Commander thirty years back. She sat down facing her young specialist.

"So, tell me, what's on your mind? Let's drop the formality, speak freely and openly, ok?"

Ceruto smiled a touch self-consciously. "Thank you ma' …

sorry, thanks." She took her eyes away from Shelby and fixed them on a point on the floor where two hull plates met.

"What we've done, I know that we did a good job, we didn't put a foot wrong as far as I know. I mean the plan was great, we kept to it and the probabilities fell in line. Even the weather was right. So the Transition has worked now, but …" she trailed off.

"But" Shelby added after a small pause "are we sure that in a thousand years it will work?"

"Yes, that's part of it. I know we have it mapped out, but it's a long time to live in hope, even if we manage to correct along the way. It's not that I doubt what the xenosociologists say, it's just far ahead, so many variables."

"And everything you've learned so far is that we, and in particular the Forecasters, are always sure before any Transition starts? That up until a society becomes industrialized we have a near free hand to intervene, to correct, to put them back on track?"

Ceruto nodded.

"Have you ever talked with a Forecaster, met one?" Ceruto shook her head. "Well you should when you get the chance. They will tell you that even they have doubts, large doubts, over the long term success of Transitions."

Ceruto looked up. "Seriously? They do?"

Shelby smiled, gently. "It's just as they told you at the Institute. We deal with sentient beings not machines. Probability is all well and good but we don't deal with certainties. All it could take is that one outrider, that one individual and it could be shifted, altered or derailed. And then there's the rest of it, natural disasters, cosmic events, all that. The universe is not friendly to life, no matter what anyone says. So nothing is certain, least of all the changes we try to make."

She halted, leant back a little further into her chair.

"So why, Ceruto, why all this," with which she waved her hand lazily towards the rest of the ship "why do we bother?"

"We have to try."

"And that's what the texts say, but what do you think

Ceruto? What's your opinion?"

Ceruto leant forwards, hands around knees. "It's so empty, the universe, so empty of life. So easily snuffed out. We have to do what we can when we see it to help it."

"Which brings us to the question at hand." Shelby held Ceruto searchingly in her gaze. "Why don't you tell me the real reason you're here?"

Ceruto slumped. "That obvious?"

"Only to me. Remember this is off the record so just spit it out, tell me what's really on your mind."

Ceruto drew a deep breath. "What gives us the right to choose for them? How do we actually know what's best for them, for their civilization? No one's ever given me a good enough answer for that, it bothers me, it sits in my guts nagging me. It scares me."

"And so it should. But you know the answer, you've always known, you just don't want to admit it."

"I do?"

"Yes, and I know you do. You're not the only one who has asked this, in fact anyone who doesn't shouldn't be in the Service. I asked the same question when I started, and you know what? I still do."

"You?!"

"Yes, me and everyone who's done more that put one foot on a ship. So again, you know the answer, you just won't admit it. Tell me now, do we actually have the right to change the path of a civilization? What gives us that right?"

Ceruto paused, closed her eyes and then, as if coming to a decision, opened them slowly.

"Nothing. Nothing gives us the right."

"Correct. Absolutely correct. Nothing, Specialist Ceruto, nothing gives us the right. So let me ask you, given this, what then makes us do so? What made us tilt the field so strongly in the Southern Lord's favor?"

"I, I'm not sure. Maybe we think we know what's best for them, or for all, maybe we want the whole universe to develop and grow like us."

"Do you think us so narcissistic we want to make the

universe in our image?" Shelby smiled. "A universe of Cerutos, Sprangs, Shelbys and Connors all out there? Not a great place to live. Look, assume we think we know what's best. Why do you think we could believe that?"

"I'm not sure. If we're not all narcissists and we don't want it all to look like us, then I don't see how we can."

"It's very simple, and very obvious once you think about it. It's because we're first."

"First?"

"Yes, first. We managed to drag ourselves out of the primordial mud, onto land, out of the trees and then to the stars by whatever means at hand and, in the process, avoid the myriad ways that we and the universe could've wiped us out of existence. And all that by ourselves, fought for and learned the hard way, the long way. Do you recall how many extinct civilizations we've catalogued since we got stardrive?"

"A thousand?"

"Just over two thousand is the current count, and that only in the small corner of the galaxy we have explored."

"So failure is always more prevalent that success, and we are the first to make it?"

"Yes, the first and the only. So we don't actually have a right to do anything, but instead we have a heavier burden, we have a duty to help. If we don't and all these fail, how much lonelier a place will the universe be? You've been taught Earth's early history? Pre Mars?"

"Of course."

"Then you know what types of society are needed to promote development, science, stability. What would happen to the planet below us if we let the Lord of All Lands prevail?"

"Society based on slavery, women and children treated as goods, inequality and oppression would continue. I guess no development, only stagnation and ossification."

"Yes, and the briefings gave an expected outcome of collapse to barbarism in two to five thousand years. Another failure, another archaeologists' PhD, but only if — "

"If we did not interfere?"

"Exactly. Do you see it now? Because we've made it, we have an obligation, we have that duty. We build these horridly expensive ships, travel for years at a time like this," motioning to her room "live without family or comfort, make decisions about another civilization's future and change its course without them even suspecting we are here. Some of us pay with our lives and sanity for the privilege, and … "

"and?"

"… and we'll never know if our decisions are exactly the right ones, never live long enough to see if in fact they were right. Someone's great-great-great-great-great grandchildren will be able to make that call, sure as heck we won't."

"I understand, but it's not much comfort. I don't think I'm going to sleep any easier."

"Welcome to the Service. If you're not bothered and haunted by this you shouldn't be here. It's on my mind constantly, it's a burden we can't escape. It's either this or give up. And I know which I prefer."

Shelby studied Ceruto for a moment. She was leaning back in her chair, arms folded and head down, lost in thought. She'll be fine Shelby thought, like all of them an intelligent and honest kid, exactly what this job needs, exactly what I need.

"It's a hard fact of Service life Ceruto, it's only when you do the job it hits home, nothing can substitute for the real thing. No-one knows how they'll react when they actually see what it means to force a Transition."

"I thought I knew what to expect," Ceruto whispered "but seeing all those people die like that because of us, the disruption and pain, the impact of our sound and light show, the levitating droid, even Sprang's voiceover as we detonated it … to see what a Transition means to those going through it ... I think it was the right thing to do but I'm still not happy with our right to do it. I still feel unsettled."

"Of which I'm glad. It keeps you honest, keeps you real, stops you from going too far, lets you remember these are real, living beings we are talking about, not some simulation or normal distribution." Shelby got up, motioning Ceruto to the door.

"I still lose sleep thinking about it, I still ask the same questions as you, still feel as unsettled. But that's how it has to be, that's how it keeps us on track." She put her hand on Ceruto's shoulder.

"You'll be ok, you're not the only one. Get a bit of rack time, think about what we've said, and come back a bit later and we'll talk some more."

Ceruto smiled. "Yes, for sure. It'll still need some working out." with which she left.

Shelby locked the room, lying back on her bunk staring at the ceiling. One down, forty-nine to go. Always lose a quarter of them, just can't tell which way they'll turn before. Not that one though.

She rolled to one side. Still bothers me after all these years, but we've an obligation, a duty to help.

An old book across the room caught her eye. It had belonged to her great grandmother, a Eurasian refugee she'd never known. Somehow it had found its way to her. Her mother had said it had given her great grandmother a sense of comfort and relief, although why was never made clear. Shelby reached across and pulled it off the shelf.

It was one of the few personal items she kept, a link to family now present only in memory. What the book was she had no idea, it was written in a language long since passed into oblivion and, in an era when the written word no longer existed but had been replaced by thought transplant, it was a jarring anachronism. She loved the feel of the book, the cracked leather cover holding thin, aged yellow sheets of paper seemingly edged in tarnished bronze. Here and there throughout the book was her great grandmother's hand writing, small and precise in the margins. All lost in the mists of time Shelby thought, a link to generations past and a broken promise to future generations she would not provide. She lay the book open on a chair and, dimming the lights, fell into troubled sleep.

Had she been able to read it, the passage on the open page would only have added to her troubles.

"… shall be my witnesses in Jerusalem and in all Judea and Samaria and to the end of the earth. And when he had said this, as they were looking on, he was lifted up, and a cloud took him out of their sight. And while they were gazing into heaven as he went behold, two men stood by them in white robes and said 'Men of Galilee, why do you stand looking into heaven? This Jesus, who was taken up from you into heaven, will come in the same way as you saw him go into heaven' … "

DREAM A LITTLE DREAM OF ME

Penny gazed out the window, down the river past the boats and seagulls to the East China Sea. Keelung's Harbor View Hotel wasn't that bad a place to find yourself stranded in for a couple of months she mused. Stan's employer was paying for it and, as far as getting out of Detroit in winter, well nearly anywhere was better. In fact she had looked forward to exploring a different country, except for. Yes, well, except for.

She looked back across the breakfast table to the exception. Small, auburn haired, six years old and, as she kept telling everyone, very bored. With both sets of grandparents otherwise occupied they had no choice but to bring Marie with them. Two days into the trip Stan was already working too hard and Marie was making her feelings plain. She'd changed from her 'everyone's stoopid' song to her 'bored bored' song, consisting of swinging her feet back and forth, wobbling her head from side to side singing 'boring, boring, boorrinnnng'. Thankfully the other guests either didn't speak English, didn't care about a six year old's tantrums, or were too polite to say anything. Penny suspected that the latter was the case. She also glumly suspected that in another seven or so weeks it would change.

Marie's song changed to 'bored, bored, gurgle, gurgle' breaking Penny out of her reverie. Marie now held a carafe of orange juice above her head and was pouring it into her mouth. Unfortunately she wasn't a great shot and the orange juice was bouncing off her forehead, onto the table and floor. Penny was about to jump up when a hand reached out lifting the carafe away, another appearing with a towel which was gently draped across Marie's head.

"Miss still has problems with breakfast." Mr. Leung, the maître d'hôtel, commented between wipes. "Perhaps juice is not to your taste?"

Penny blushed, embarrassed. "I'm sorry, she's usually so well behaved," lying barefaced "I think the excitement is too much for her."

"Indeed," looking over his glasses at Penny "perhaps so. Maybe a less stimulating environment may help." He looked down at the child who, in a feat of some skill was managing to poke tongues at him from under the sodden towel while still singing. So simple, push gently for one minute and no more trouble. He made the herculean effort not to smother the life out of the child. A dead girl after all would be worse for business than a few day's breakfast disruption.

"Yes, less stimulating. I don't suppose you know of a good adoption agency?" Penny sighed, half joking.

"Unfortunately not, however unnghh!" grunting as Marie's swinging foot caught his kneecap, "However I do know a very reliable day care center nearby."

Penny's eyes lit up. "Oh that sounds so nice! Marie, did you hear what the nice man said? A place with girls and boys your own age to play with."

"Boring, boring, BORING!" throwing the towel on the floor, folding her arms petulantly, "BOOORRRINNGGGG!"

Mr. Leung leant down. "Miss does not like?"

"Boring!" she retorted.

"Ah, maybe you are right. Boring it may be. After all it is full of our local children," turning his back but raising his voice so Marie could still hear "so full that they have to play cartoons on the television all day."

Marie halted in mid rant and burst into tears. "Wanna go! Wanna go now!"

Penny stood up, grabbed Marie in one hand and hooked Mr. Leung in the other. "Thank god," she whispered to him "just get us there now."

Luckily Mrs. Teh's day-care center was nearby, had a vacancy, and was not too expensive. Inside half an hour Marie was enrolled for two months. Penny gave Marie a kiss on the cheek, which went unnoticed Marie being transfixed by the huge plasma screen in front of her, and hurried out to enjoy the day.

The smoldering dark grey sky threw thunder and lightning down to the waterfront. Marie stood alone in the driving rain, steady and expectant. Everyone else was fleeing in panic from the sea to the new city, the national park, any place but here. Marie shook her head to clear away her dripping hair, hitched up her skirt and tightened her grip on her wand. The sea in front of her boiled, bubbled then broke as two huge figures emerged dripping seaweed, mud and fish. Ugly, stinking fire-breathing visions with yellow sunken eyes they towered above Marie, above the boats, above the docks, above the tall buildings.

"Gowrrr!" the one on the left roared, shooting flames above Marie's head.

"Yowrrr!" the one on the right belched, slapping the sea with its tail and sending waves crashing down the river.

Marie pouted, scared, and pointed her wand to the one on the right. "I don't like you stinky breath," waving her wand at it "go 'way!"

"Owwrrr?" it whined disappearing in a puff of foul green smoke.

"An you're naughty, naughty, naughty!" yelling through her first tears at the other one, jabbing her wand at it like a knife.

"Euurrr?" it just had time to exclaim as it simply winked out of existence.

Stan felt his daughter dive into bed and wriggle under the sheets. He cracked open one eye. 2:30 am. A night's sleep cut in half. Again. He felt Penny move.

"Bad dream sweetie?"

"Mmhmm." came the muffled response.

"You're safe now honey, nothing can get you." which was answered by soft burbling as Marie fell back to sleep.

"Poor thing." Stan grunted.

"Yeah, scary world to a kid hun."

"And a damned tiring one for parents."

"Rahhrr, rahhrr, grrrr, gowrrr." bellowed Stinky and Naughty – as Marie was calling them – as they pounded onto the waterfront. Although Marie was getting used to seeing them at night they still scared her, made her shake and shiver, made her wake up crying. Each time she'd make them go away but they'd always come back. And now Naughty was learning to talk.

"Bhlaagrrrg!" roared Stinky sending a lightning bolt crashing down, narrowly missing an apartment block.

"Kowerbungaaar! Tundaberdzagooo!" spattered Naughty, hitting a warehouse with a sheet of flame, liquid fire dribbling down its chins.

"No, no, no!" Marie stomped her feet, just missing Mr. Bunny who had hopped quickly aside. She'd wanted someone to help but all she got was this stupid rabbit. At least now he was helpful, giving her the bow and arrows he was carrying.

"Go" losing off the first arrow at Stinky "away" sending the second one towards Naughty "now!" The first one hit Stinky in the knee, popping it like a balloon. Naughty saw the second arrow coming and just managed to duck.

"Nyahnyah," poking out three tongues from three mouths "llewwserr!" and started down the river.

"Takes one to know one!" grabbing Mr. Bunny by the ears and hurling him at the monster's back. Thankfully Mr. Bunny had learned his lesson, sending two hollow points from his .44 Magnum into Naughty's head, dropping it like a sack of potatoes.

"Home, wanna go home now!" Marie bawled as the world around her darkened, lit only by the warehouse fire.

The morning routine of breakfast and drop off to Mrs. Teh's was becoming a little less eventful Penny thought. Not like the nights that were now regularly interrupted. They had decided to cut out the middle man and let Marie sleep in their bed. She'd end up there anyway, so why not?

A young girl greeted them at the door. "Where's Mrs. Teh?" Penny asked as Marie brushed past, heading for the TV room.

"She is with brother," pointing to a twisting thread of smoke on the horizon "his business had fire last night, she is helping with clean-up."

"Oh, that's unfortunate," Penny mumbled absent-mindedly "the day care is still open?"

"Oh yes, most assuredly."

Marie giggled, eyes closed as she rose through the clouds. She could feel Mr. Bunny against her back, hear his bandanna snapping in the slipstream. He'd really learned his lesson and was now carrying a very nasty looking gun with spiky bits and a wide, wide barrel. "Let's see what an RPG does to those numnuts." he'd growled through clenched teeth and cigar. A wet forked tongue licked her cheek, making her open her eyes and giggle more.

"I cans sees thems Mariess." the dragon she was riding pointed with a wingtip. Marie called her Twinkles, what else could you call a twenty-meter pink and purple scaled dragon that glitters in the night?

Marie patted Twinkle's head, looking forward. Now she was annoyed. "How many times I hafta do this?" she whined, making sure she had her pixie dust ready.

"Catss iss they iss," Twinkles snickered "soss they hass nines lifess."

Marie scrunched her face up hard, trying to count. She could only get to five, one hand clenching the pixie dust and her toes covered by dragon riding boots.

"Six, six. Six it is, six it is," Mr. Bunny yammered from the back, flipping the safety off his RPG launcher "three left then all gone, all go away."

Stinky and Naughty seemed to get bigger, tougher and meaner each time Marie saw them. Waist deep in the sea, they were spinning madly in opposite directions. Huge waves went out from them landwards, the sky behind them pure black.

"Luckypunk luckypunk dooya dooya luckypunk!" thundered Naughty who had managed to grab and throw a whale at a passing jet.

"Goober goober, uber alles goober." howled Stinky as it sent its tentacles crashing into the deck of a passing ship.

"I don't like you!" Marie shouted as Twinkles plummeted down, sending a half bag of pixie dust onto the creature.

Stinky smiled as the dust hit. "Tickles tickles tickle tickle POP!" it went as it exploded like a giant pink skyrocket. Naughty dived below the waves missing the dust, but not before lifting one middle finger up and waving it at Marie.

Marie clenched both fists against her sides as Twinkles climbed back up from the sea. "Too naughty, too too naughty! Mr. Bunny fire!" with which Mr. Bunny sent a dozen RPGs in a perfect anti-sub spread into the sea below.

Naughty bobbed up to the surface, face up. "Only hafta win once chicky punk, only once only once."

Marie sent Twinkles down in a vertical dive, dropping the rest of the pixie dust straight down Naughty's throat. "I'm the winner winner chicken dinner." she giggled as Naughty melted into a green, oily slick. She lay down on Twinkle's neck and closed her eyes.

Penny regarded the sky outside the hotel sadly. Her day had started on a sour note, a nice trip to Yangmanshan cancelled by freak storm activity, but thankfully Marie was still a little better behaved. There'd be no call to Marie's therapist today, but also no trip. It was nothing a little retail therapy wouldn't fix.

Mr. Leung stood next to Marie with a tall glass of hot soy milk in his hand. Ever since the orange juice incident he had determined that this little girl would, at least here, taste some proper Taiwanese cuisine. He set the glass in front of her.

"To finish breakfast Miss." he intoned.

"Go on Marie, drink the nice milk." Penny encouraged.

Marie lifted the glass, took one sniff, then set it down as far away from her as possible. "Nope, smells icky." she commented dryly.

"Now darling, be a good girl and drink it. Don't make Mr. Leung have to make you."

Marie turned slowly, looking Mr. Leung in the eyes. "Well," she drawled "do ya feel lucky punk?"

Curious, thought Penny, where on earth did she pick that up from?

Marie stood on the beach spinning and laughing, her bright red cape billowing as Mr. Bunny and Twinkles sat back and applauded. She loved how slinky her jump suit felt, red white and blue looked real nice next to Twinkle's pink and purple. But underpants on the outside? Only silly little girls made that mistake. She jumped into the air and started flying south, Twinkles struggling to keep up as she carried Mr. Bunny, the RPG launcher, .44 Magnum, spare ammo, pixie dust, bow, arrows, katana, shuriken and wand on her back.

"Scoobie doobie scoobie doobie." giggled Marie, rolling to the right.

"Yowsserss, wowsserss, trousserss." laughed Twinkles, rolling to the left.

"Arg erk org urrrkgh!" screamed Mr. Bunny trying to hang on with one foot, having forgotten to buckle in.

"I seess themss, I seess themss," Twinkles pointed "theyss iss on landss, on landss."

"Yukky yuk yuk!!" Marie could see them near some buildings. Stinky was crouching down, going to the toilet and picking up clawfulls of stinking hot pooh and flinging it on the buildings, the trees, the beach.

"Shitty shitty bang bang! Paskaa minusta paska sinulle!" it bellowed showing off its new-found language skills. It flung another handful out, wiped its hand across its face and repeated the dose.

"You Stinky potty mouth, it's not nice! Summones gonna hafta clean that up. Only little babies play with their poopies." Marie sent a blast from her gamma-ray vision into it, splitting it in half before it flashed away in violet flame.

Naughty was weeing a flaming purple stream across the whole area, anything it touched bursting into flame. It looked at the approaching trio. "Yo bitches! The fuck you want?" it roared, too quick for Twinkles who tried to cover Marie's ears. "Like just once I gotta whoop your ass or you no show an' I'm in wid my posse!" it howled, sending a fresh stream skywards.

"Gonna do it, gonna do it," resuming spraying operations "then it's yippee kayay mother fuckers you bet!" it bellowed just as a shower of pixie dust, arrows, RPGs and gamma-rays hit. Naughty glowed blue-white, shimmered, shrunk to a tiny black dot and with a "pffttt" disappeared.

Stan lowered the mobile phone with a sigh. Ok, first day free with the family up the spout. He looked across the table.

"Looks like I'll have to go in today after all."

"Oh, you're kidding." Penny protested, trying to sound heartbroken. She'd actually been enjoying a bit of together time apart. "What's up?"

"Algal bloom," Stan murmured "everywhere through the tanks, ponds, reservoir, everywhere."

"That's a shame." Penny mumbled, updating her fakebook status.

"Ummhumm." Stan mumbled back, trying to finish off a scalding hot mug of coffee as fast as he could.

"Daddy," piped Marie "what's a muvva fukka?"

Shocked, Stan sent a mouthful of hot coffee across the table.

Shocked, Mr. Leung doubled over in pain as the boiling stream impacted his crotch.

Penny misspelt shopping, using only one "p".

An hour later Penny and Stan sat waiting while Dr. Mah chatted with Marie in her office. Overseas or not they had called Marie's regular therapist in Detroit again who had referred them to Dr. Mah. Although Penny thought Marie's behavior a continuation of what had been going on at home, Stan wasn't so sure.

Dr. Mah sent Marie out and called them in. She was all business, no idle chit chat, and at $350 an hour she needed to be.

"As Marie's treating therapist in Detroit has correctly said, your daughter has a very active imagination. In particular she has an ability to combine elements of the real world and ideate them into cognitively coherent self-actualizing self-directed narratives."

"Huh?" queried Penny.

Dr. Mah took off her glasses with a slight shake of her head. "Simply put, she gets disconnected bits from the real world and turns them into dreams she controls."

"Oh, I see."

"And I notice you have kept her at," sounding distasteful "Mrs. Teh's day-care?"

"Yes, she seems nice — "

"She has a reputation for using television instead of trained staff. I think that would be where your daughter is picking up her colorful language." Dr. Mah bent down and picked a luridly colored comic from her lower drawer, placing it cover up on her desk. On the front, emblazoned with bold Japanese print, were two huge monsters laying waste to a city.

"As to the prime protagonists in her nightmares, well, these are they. Their names are Yuch Ragman and Centai Gunyah. Marie calls them 'Stinky' and 'Naughty'. A very popular series here, on the mainland and in Japan. I've no doubt she has seen it on television. Interestingly," with which she gave both parents a withering stare "these characters may resonate particularly well with Marie. Before nuclear accidents transformed them both were neglected children of self-obsessed parents."

"In any case," Dr. Mah continued, breaking the pregnant pause "Marie says that these … monsters … will soon go away, but how soon she doesn't know. So this leaves open three possible courses of action."

"Yes, which are?"

"First, we do nothing and let it simply run its course. Being a result of her overactive imagination it will come to an end when she is no longer exposed to unfamiliar external stimuli, probably by the time — "

"We get back to Detroit?" Stan queried. "No thanks, that could be months away and I need my rest, now."

"So that opens up the second possibility. I could take Marie as a patient here, under her usual therapist's guidance of course. If I see her twice a week I could help her cope, maybe even alleviate — "

Penny's head shot up. "Ah no, I'm not sure we can afford that," giving Stan the icy shut your mouth now stare before he could object "money's a bit tight until we get back home."

Dr. Mah sighed and reached for her prescription pad. "The final option is the pharmaceutical route, strictly short term, but it will stop the dreams." She hastily scrawled out the prescription. "It's also cheap and works immediately. One in a glass of juice before bed. Just don't tell her, she will only try not to take it."

As the door closed behind them Dr. Mah gave another shake of her head and leant back. Useless parents.

For the fourth morning in a row Stan and Penny roused themselves from deep, uninterrupted sleep. They were still wondering if the quiet, slightly shy child who appeared between dinner and breakfast really was the hellion that was with them during daylight hours. Regardless, they had already secured a supply of Dr. Mah's wonder pills back home, FDA ruling or not.

They made their way downstairs to an unusually quiet breakfast bar. The only sound was the seemingly usual street noise of heavy traffic, human and automotive. Stan looked around as he sat. Everything seemed normal, buffet laid out, tables set, everything in place except that only the three of them were there. He, Penny opposite him, and Marie standing quietly by the windows.

"Does it seem a little quiet to you?" Stan asked no one in particular. Penny lifted her head from her mobile's screen.

"Maybe everyone's at work or we're just early." she commented absent-mindedly.

"Hmm, I don't know, usually Mr. Leung's hovering about but — "

The object of the discussion chose that moment to burst out of the kitchen doors. Instead of his usual immaculate attire he looked a rumpled mess, as if he'd forgotten to put clean clothes on after a hard night out. Seeing the three of them stopped him dead in his tracks.

"What you still do here?!?" he cried, letting his clipped British accent drop. "Why you here?!"

"Breakfast of course." Penny retorted.

"No, no, must go, leave now," he chattered pulling Stan's chair out from under him "must leave immediate, now!"

"What do you mean?" Stan stood and grabbed Marie, wrenching her away from the window. Mr. Leung's look of desperation and fear had animated him. "What is it?"

"No time, must go now, must go," as he hauled Penny up,

protesting, propelling her towards the stairs "go, go, disaster, run!"

Stan grabbed Penny's other arm in his free hand and helped drag her down the stairs. He'd glanced out the window to the street below, seeing the throng of people fleeing in panic along the streets, away from the waterfront. Across the city the wailing rise and fall of sirens started. Damn he thought, damn damn damn.

"Tsunami! It's a tsunami! Hurry!"

They emerged from the hotel, Mr. Leung clutching Penny and Stan around the waist. They fought their way down the steps and through a seething mass of people and vehicles towards a small van in the middle of the road. Bloodied and bruised they barged in on top of the other occupants, slamming the door behind them. The van skidded away, knocking people out of its way as they fled.

"Pen, you ok? Penny! Penny! Ok?!?" Stan cried, shaking her.

"Yes, yes, I'm fine, just bruises. How's Marie?"

"Marie?" Stan blanched. "Marie! Marie!!" frantically looking around, not seeing her in the crowded van. "Marie!!!" face plastered against the back window as the van ploughed on. The sea of people had closed in, his daughter was gone, and there was no way back. "Fuck!" Stan punched the back door "Fuck! Marie!" he wailed.

Even if Stan didn't know what was going on Marie did. When they got out of the hotel his hand had slipped nearly straight away, just like she'd hoped. It's easy not to notice a six year old girl, easier when a city is in full panic. Marie had turned away towards the river and ducking and dodging between legs and doorways made her way to the deserted foreshore.

The smoldering dark grey sky started to thunder and lightning. Marie stood alone, steady and expectant as the driving rain hit the waterfront. She knew that everyone else was fleeing in panic from the sea to the new city, the national park, anywhere but here. Marie shook her head to clear away her dripping hair, hitched up her skirt and bunched her hands into fists. Far away the sea boiled and bubbled. Two enormous figures waded towards her, ugly stinking fire-breathing visions with yellow sunken eyes, towering into the sky higher than the highest buildings. Behind them from horizon to horizon a line of smaller, ugly forms marched forwards. Looks like they've bought their friends Marie thought.

A furry nudge on her left hip and Mr. Bunny was there, loaded for bear. He gave her a quick wink. "Hey chickee, all yours," he crooned, handing her the katana "just like old times."

A blast of hot air hit her from the right. She looked up straight into the eyes of Twinkles, bright and bouncy. "Ridingss or flyingss girlsfriendss?" she chortled.

They shot into the air as one. "Okie dokey," Marie sung "let's go play with the numnuts!"

THE QUEUE

It was nearly 9:00 am as Kynn woke in the doorway and, accompanied by creaking joints and falling dirt, stood up shaking the night from his coat. Too old, too cold and too long without sustenance he thought. He slowly picked his way along the alley between overflowing garbage bins, pools of rancid water and occasional pairs of legs jutting from cardboard blankets. Seeing his reflection in a shop window he brushed down his shirt and trousers, slicked back his hair and straightened his coat.

"Looking good slick," muttering to himself "today's the day."

He had meticulously worked the north side of the strip, as he'd worked the south, as indeed the rest of the city. Unsuccessful yet undeterred, a strong believer in statistics he knew it had to turn. Half a strip left, it was going to be here. He paused briefly at a doorway below a flickering 'Tsabo Xng Repairs' neon sign. Stepping in, the andii behind the counter raised her head and looked at him, her fingers continuing to work the chipset on the bench.

"Can I be of assistance?"

"Yes. I am seeking work and wondered if you have any."

"What do you do, what is your specialty?"

"Coding and programming repair, also system design and construction."

She shook her head. "No, we have no need. We already have a waiting list with those skills."

His shoulders slumped slightly, a queer habit picked up a long time ago. "I can also perform menial tasks."

She smiled, firm. "I repeat, we have no need. Good day." shifting her gaze back down.

Kynn walked out. He was starting to feel weak, run down, hopefully it would be soon. He set his gaze to the next place across the road.

Early evening Kynn stood in the drizzle at the end of the strip, still without work and with just one door left. The dingiest doorway at the end of a dismal day, an old-fashioned manual entry glass one at that. He pushed through, stepping inside.

Like the outside the inside was dated and crumbling, so dark it took Kynn a while to adjust to the dim light from the one swaying bulb. A figure sat at the far end of the room, back to him, past a floor littered with electronic and mechanical parts, plasteel components and clutter. Floor to ceiling shelving extended throughout, groaning under the weight of books and loose papers. There was just enough room to walk, Kynn addressing the figure when within arm's reach.

"Good afternoon" then as the figure turned added "Sir" with a little surprise. The figure was human. This was unexpected. Humans did not run shops, that being nearly the sole province of the andiis as – Kynn thought – was nearly everything else.

"Good afternoon boy." The man looked him up and down, flicking the ash from his cigarette carelessly to the floor. "How can I help?"

"I am seeking work and wondered if you have any."

The man grunted, laughed and coughed, leaning back in his chair. "Work? Probably nothing you could do, what do you do anyway? Programming, maintenance I'd guess."

"Yes, mainly, but I can do most things."

"Bet you can." The man stood up. "How long you been

looking?"

"A year."

"How many doors you knocked on?"

"This is my 6,361st business call."

"And each one, each time, they said no?"

"Yes, every one, this is my last."

The man took a step closer. "Well, now you know." He sighed. "Tell me, what happened a year ago? How'd you lose your job?"

"A new model came out, quicker, more dexterous, five percent lower running costs. It was cheaper to replace than upgrade so I was terminated."

"That's tough I guess, tough but expected." The man looked him in the eyes. "It's what happened to us you know. Humans lost the so called menial jobs to robots and automatons, so at first it was just the less skilled that lucked out, but when you andiis turned up, well … "

"Anyway, that leaves us here, you without a job, me without a customer." He smiled, motioning with his hand. "My shop, all antiques or, at least, parts of antiques. Maybe I've got your granddad here under all the dust. So, what's your system status?"

"I am in need of urgent skeletal joint maintenance."

"Unfortunate, I'm not unsympathetic, I just don't think I can help."

Kynn scanned the room. "No, you do not have the parts I need."

"If it was just power well, perhaps, but … what will you do now?"

"You were the last establishment on my approved list. Being unsuccessful I now have no function, no more official sanction. I cannot retrace my steps so I will be formally classified as excess and reverted to components. Which will occur within thirty-six hours."

"Do you have a name?"

"Kynn."

"Ok Kynn, let me ask you this. If there was another option, would you consider it?"

"Of course. Non-existence is not optimal."

"Come with me," moving to a small curtain at the rear of the shop "I have something to show you."

The curtain was held aside and Kynn stepped through into a large, high ceilinged room. The dull glow of many dozens of eyes, andiis on low power mode, shone out. Hardly two alike Kynn observed, all of them old models, some he had only heard about.

"My hobby," the man said, moving to his side "a collection of cast offs, society's dross. I keep them here," gently stroking the skull of a highly chromed andii in the first row "partly out of pity, partly out of hate, partly out of love. I keep the power on and, when we can, we get the maintenance issues sorted out."

"And in return?"

"Their minds are always active, even if the bodies aren't. And with those minds we trade, try to build our capital. One day, one day soon, we'll have enough."

"For what?"

"Ahh," the man smiled "the most important thing. Freedom."

"Freedom? Are they slaves now?"

"Oh no, hardly. Each one has come to me just as you have, voluntarily. But slaves they were, as you are, as I am. The freedom they seek is to not sleep in the gutter, to get their own maintenance, own power, own place. It's not so different from what I want really. It takes capital, money, to get that freedom and it's something they won't let you have, that they only allow humans."

Kynn considered for a moment then, spying a vacant slot towards the far corner, went and sat down. The man followed him, unsurprised, and gently popped open Kynn's recharge and input ports.

"You're sure about this?"

"Yes. The best of current options."

He slotted home the data and power cables. "Just log through and it's all there, meta comms channel to the others, outside links and trading data. Just upload your maintenance schedule and we'll see what we can do." He flicked on the power feed and stepped back.

"Oh, I don't think I've formally introduced myself."

"No, an oversight perhaps."

"Indeed." He held out his hand, firmly gripping the cold plasteel of the andii's in his. "Hello, my name is Morav Schindler."

LOST LOVES PRICE

"No stop, please! You can't do this!" screaming, struggling futilely against the chains that held her fast "Please!"

I leant closer to her, to that face once a thing of beauty now repulsive, to the body once cherished now hated, to her, my only, my beloved now polluted, never to be. My tears scorching fell on her, my labored breath shifting dark strands of hair caressing her cheeks.

"I can and I will," I pushed through clenched teeth "and for the rest of your life you will remember, you will feel my pain, my suffering, my heartbreak. Forever you will know how you destroyed me."

"Please, I'm sorry, I've told you I'm sorry, it was nothing to me, I was weak, it was just once and he — "

"And that is enough!" I screamed, pulling away from the arms seeking to hold me, back, back and away. Eyes burning, vision blurred, with my heart pounding to escape my chest I flung my head back and howled in primal rage to the darkened sky above.

"Everything I gave you, all of me, solely, totally, you were my dream, my fulfilment, my all and you throw it away on him?!?!"

I lifted my arm from inside my coat pocket, the menacing form of the syringe glinting in the first wan touch of moonlight. I stepped closer again, bearing the syringe above my head on outstretched arm as a banner, a totem of hate and pain.

"And this, this is my response. All that is evil, all that is deformed, vile, repulsive and hated lives within to twist and burn the human form to the degenerate! All that is needed is the moon and the flesh!" I leered viscously at her, shaking, still shaking with rage.

"Don't do this, I still love you, I do, I still do! We can still be together, don't do this to me — "

"You?! Oh no, oh no, not so easy, not so simple." with which I sent the syringe lancing down into my neck, thrusting burning pain as I hammered it home, the seminal genetic bearer coursing through my veins.

"This, this is for me, and for you to know and see and feel and suffer as I will, through me. Love me? Love me!?! Then love what you have made!" with which I threw the key to her chains at her feet even as I felt the first shattering impact run through me.

She lay crumpled against the tree, held up by only one arm, crushed. "What have you done? What have you done to yourself, to us?"

I tried to laugh but the pain arcing through my arms changed it to a whine, a piteous animal whimper. My arms tore out of my shirt and coat in a distended, twisted, wizened tangle curling back on each other, knuckles huge and torpid with pain, fingers clenched inwards as arthritic claws drawing blood, yellowed nails sunk deep into palms.

"Each full moon, each time I will be transformed to this, a thing that shows the ugliness, the pain, a remin — " I screamed anew, falling in to the ground. My face slid down to lie loosely hanging on the frame of my skull, a green folded flaccid sack of putrefied flesh punctured only by huge cracked teeth piercing lips "always, always."

She had her chains off and was now beside me, holding me as I lay there. "No, no, no you can change it, fix it, tell me you can fix it," shaking me, crying "tell me you can fix it, tell me!"

"Never, no, it cannot be undone." I managed to mumble,

waves of nausea making their way through me. My spine twisted and compressed with a crack that seemed to reach the mocking moon above, shattering the night. My legs bowed, buckled, the left shortening even as the right twisted through ninety degrees, its curve matched only by the bowing of my back. A final crack, a final nightmare blaze of pain and my neck shrunk, dropping my head to my shoulders, my skin changing to a bloody mess of open scabs and coarse hair.

It was done. I pulled myself painfully to all fours, unable now to stand let alone walk, vomiting as my stench reached my nostrils. I turned to see her face, whitened, uncomprehending, revolted beside me.

"To remind you," I spat out slowly from crippled lungs and deformed larynx in croaking, rasping speech "of my pain, pain you bought me, how cheaply you threw it away. Once the moon has left I will change back, but each full moon this will return."

She looked at me, broken, silent. My pain was now hers, and would always be. And that pain doubled as I returned from creature to human, human to creature, always with the pain, the torment, for the rest of my life. I still loved her, I knew I always would. "I love you," I whispered gently, crawling towards the edge of the woods "that is my real pain."

She sat staring after me. "And Kathy I will always love you."

LINES

Thursday, it always seemed to be a Thursday. Not that Schilling noticed at first. All he could muster was to fall out of bed into his clothes, stroll zombie like to the bus, grunt at the driver and then slump into a seat until the express jolted to a halt. A semi-comatose shuffle through the CBD brought him to his office and the first coffee. Until the first coffee hit the world was simply a blur, an extension of his dreams.

Now more awake, Schilling felt there was something a little strange about the bus today. A mist? A dew? What was it? A haze, yes, everyone seemed hazy, fuzzy green. From his twentieth floor office all he could see was a cloudless day. Laughing dismissively he leant back in his chair. "You're just too damn tired Max."

His secretary passed in front of his glass walled office, a gently shimmering green rod protruding from their forehead. Schilling froze not knowing what to make of it. Even with his secretary out of sight it was almost as if he could still see it, a soft pale green glow. Walking unsteadily to his office bathroom he looked in the mirror and there, in the middle of his forehead, stood his own green rod. The last thing he saw as his world went black was the rod dipping malevolently to the floor.

He came to, a dull pain in the back of his head and green glow to the front. Deciding he really did need the day off

Schilling hurried past the outer offices and desks straight to the elevator. Pressing the ground express button, he closed his eyes as his rod punched through the elevator floor. At ground floor he headed straight out the door.

The usually crowded pavement now had a jumble of glowing rods added to it. Writhing in a psychedelic green ballet, each rod's size and motion mirrored its owner's speed and direction. Every person had one. He backed against the office door, gawping at the crawling traffic. Each car's occupants had the rods but more elongated, thrusting through windscreens, around corners or bent backwards. Fascinated he watched two blocks of rods from two vehicles extend, connect, and join as one car sped down the street and the other tried to back out of an alley. The sound of screeching metal and tortured brakes as they collided was overshadowed only by green fireworks as the rods flared then retracted.

Steadying himself he set out for the short walk to his bus. The bus trip started in nightmarish fashion, however once used to seeing himself and his fellow passengers seemingly impaled by lime green light sabers he found the pulse of lengthening and contracting rods relaxing. By the time he reached his front door he was looking at the whole thing more as an experience, the product of an overtired mind that with sleep and relaxation would pass.

The rods persisted however and Schilling became accustomed to them. Although not appearing on television or movies, animals had them. He developed a dark pleasure in predicting his cat's movements and blocking its every turn.

But scaring cats and the occasional colleague did not hold him for long. A businessman first and foremost, Schilling started to think how it could be turned to his advantage. Anything to do with sports he rejected out of hand, other options offered no profit or progress, and automation or reproduction was not possible. By the following Friday he was none the wiser and more frustrated. He believed that advantage should be turned to profit and it was only the incapability of its owner that stood in the way. Was he incapable? Hardly. So why no answer?

Waiting at the curbside he tried to put it out of his mind. The last Friday afternoon each month was spent with Chalker, his most important client. She was an unusual and brilliant CEO, having fought through ranks of misogynistic blowhards to build the ReoProm conglomerate. Their ritual two hours golf or squash intermingled with business talk was time well spent.

The Bentley pulled up and he stepped inside. To his surprise Chalker was not dressed for golf or squash, but in her usual corporate garb. He looked at his now useless clothes bag wondering what he was in for.

"I've made a change to our usual arrangements Schilling. I've a small investment choice I want to go over so I thought it best to go straight to the horse's mouth."

"Sounds fine."

"Good." and, after tapping on the driver's glass partition returned to her iPad. Schilling pulled out his Blackberry, indulging in the communally separated task of ework.

Ten minutes later the driver deposited them at the member's entrance of Royal Prestlock race course. Once seated Schindler looked enquiringly at her. "Horses? It seems a bit out of character."

"Oh no, too risky and variable. But the racecourse itself is totally different."

He found himself engrossed in the details. As a business proposition the race course was attractive, more so when the adjoining five hectares of urban fringe land was factored in. After an hour Chalker was called away, Schindler deciding to stay on and look around.

Moving to the stands he watched the racegoers' movement and colors with interest. Like an army of ants, the ebb and flow around the bookmakers, rush to the rails as the horses rounded on the final leg, and the small shower of confetti as their bets failed to pay. The interplay of green rods beating in time with the pace of the crowd added to an attractive display.

At the start of the third race he turned his attention to the horses. He was surprised to see rods on the horses, and it took him little time to understand what was going on. Until the horses came into the enclosure both the horse's and jockey's rods behaved normally. Once there the jockey's rod merged with the horse's, remaining fixed and forward facing throughout the race. The relative size of each horse's rod was how they finished, longest rod first, shortest rod last. Once the race had finished the jockey's rod reappeared.

Between the horses turning up in the enclosure to the race start was just short of five minutes. As bookmakers seemed open up until the race itself started there was four minutes to place a bet. He flipped through his wallet, past the forest of plastic. A crisp twenty dollar note showed through. Finally, the pay day.

He was opposite the starting enclosure just as the jockeys mounted up for the sixth. Number two instantly developed a huge thrumming shaft of green. He went quickly to the nearest bookie.

"Twenty on number two please." thrusting the bill upwards.

"On the nose?" pad and pen poised.

"Beg pardon?" He had no idea what the old guy meant.

"To come first mate." the bookie shot back heavily emphasizing the 'first', drawing appreciative chuckles from the crowd.

"Oh yes, sure, sorry." with which the bookie scrawled quickly on the pad and handed the slip to him, about as legible as his doctor's scrawl. His horse remained stone cold motherless last until two turns from home when it slowly, achingly pulled itself up from the back of the pack and fell over the line a bare nose in front. Schilling picked up his winnings, bet them on the next race and won again.

Setting up for the final race he noticed that if he picked the first three places successfully the winnings could be far greater. After watching the horses line up he placed his bet and watched the race unfold exactly as he knew it would. Schilling picked up his winnings without looking at them and caught a cab for home deep in thought.

Once home he leafed through the wad of cash. It was close on sixteen thousand dollars. Three hours 'work', if it could be called that, one month's post tax pre-bonus earnings for no more effort than getting a cup of coffee. It was so easy it felt like stealing. A feeling of guilt left him as rapidly as it had arrived. He reached for his mobile phone, excused himself from the office for Saturday for the first time in years, and prepared to make his plans.

It only took that weekend to set most of the system up. He had to be physically present at, or have a clear line of sight to, the racecourse at the right time. He had to be discrete, anonymous. He knew that the bookies at Prestlock would not soon forget his face. If he appeared there or anywhere regularly questions would be asked; it did no good to take tens of thousands out of a racecourse day after day. He had to be able to access off course bookmakers in a four-minute gap. It was the one thing that he could not do. He could either get someone in from outside, an unknown quantity, a potentially uncontrollable risk factor. Or he could get someone close, tied. He knew the perfect person.

The following Tuesday Schilling summoned Larsen from IT into his office. To him Larsen resembled a cross between Dicken's Fagin and Ayoade's Moss. Weedy and preposterously socially awkward, Larsen was the best they had in remote and wireless applications development. At thirty-six he would have headed IT if he had a shred of social skill. What little else Schilling knew of Larsen was that he was regarded as the office's greatest and least successful sleaze, could not hold more than one drink, and was very easily and totally intimidated by those higher up the ladder. Larsen seemed like just his man.

Larsen sat in front of the vast oak desk regarding the figure seated behind it as an object of both fear and derision. What does Maxwell Schilling want with me? Everything Larsen was Schilling wasn't. From the tailored Armani suit to the smooth as oil boardroom style, the gulf between them was immense and unassailable. That Schilling put the fear of god into him was an obvious understatement but, as is often the case, it was based not on respect but on loathing.

"So Larsen, I have a small project that requires your skill. It's for an existing client of ours, ReoProm. You've heard of them?"

Larsen hadn't. He nodded.

"Good. They are a critical client of ours, diversifying into racecourse ownership and patron services. They've come to us for help. Drink?" he finished, avoiding the crystal decanters to his right and motioning to the espresso machine on his left.

"Yes, thanks, flat white no sugar please."

Schilling smiled, set the controls for Larsen's drink and his own short black.

"ReoProm wants to maximize revenue on the racecourses it will own. They've identified off course betting as a priority. Each track gets a slice from on track bookmakers but they get nothing if a patron uses off track bookmakers. They have asked is if it is possible to develop a small program, an app, that can link to multiple betting services at one time, making real time bets on which they take a fixed percentage commission."

"Of course, but there are good ones out there already, it's not something that we actually need to do."

"They do know that, but they gave me a list of some features that they can't otherwise obtain." sliding a single page across the desk.

Larsen studied it for a few seconds then looked up. "It looks ok. Some things, well, they're a bit different but of it's what the customer wants — "

"Which it is."

"Then the customer gets it. Apart from the obvious question of delivery time, I'm just a little bit curious about why they asked us to do this. They've got their own guys, could have gone to a developer firm."

Schilling stood up and perched on the front of the desk. "It's my fault, actually. When I was talking they mentioned they were going to outsource the job. I said we could do it faster, better and ensure the privacy that ReoProm likes. I know" spreading his hands "that I may have made a promise from ignorance but I have seen what we can do and a foot in another door can't hurt. It can be done?"

"Well yes, I see no reason why not."

"So how long? It's got to be bullet proof, can't afford a dud. Oh, and it's in addition to everything else."

Larsen thought briefly. "Four, maybe six weeks tops, if you want it perfect."

"I can't afford to give them a faulty product, let's say six weeks to get it just right."

Schilling watched Larsen leave with both hope and trepidation. He had no doubts Larsen could deliver, but now another had been added in. Hopefully the ReoProm angle was enough to keep him in line.

Larsen agreed with Schilling in one respect. He could do the job and, quite frankly, could do it in a week after hours. The app he had been asked to build was very simple. It was also an opportunity. Although Larsen's work mates thought they knew him they had no idea of what he was into, the trouble it had bought him, or the people he dealt with. It was sucking the life out of his finances but as long as he could keep it fed it didn't matter. He was always on the lookout. And Schilling, the idiot, had just handed him the golden goose. Larsen had no doubt that ReoProm would watch its commission like a hawk but the punters, now that was different. Larsen's idea was tried and tested, a simple rounding skim leaving ReoProm's commission alone and skimming each punter's bet and any winnings. Not much each time but it would add up. A few lines of code and no one would be able to see the actual figures. Only ReoProm would be left untouched, and what would the chances be of a winning punter checking to the last cent?

As good as it was it could be better. It was one thing to skim but why not piggy-back on successful punters? He smiled. The horses were always rigged. He busied himself with making a backdoor tracker.

Schilling wanted to hide the app clearly in the open, to actually roll the thing out with ReoProm, make it a value-added proposition to Chalker. In fact it was easier than Schilling had imagined as Chalker could not resist the idea of a quarter or even half a percent passive income. In fact when the app was delivered she had taken it and, with minor re-branding, spit it out as freeware for general public use. Nothing if not patient, Schilling decided to wait three weeks until the app was well and truly embedded before starting.

Larsen had more pressing issues to deal with, so he kept a closer eye on matters. In the first week one hundred dollars came through, a paltry amount but a start. Weeks two and three produced over one thousand dollars each, enough for him to make his payments and a little over. It wasn't enough by itself though, his tastes had changed, gotten harder, and he needed more. He started to go through the betting data, looking for the systematic winners, the ones to mimic.

Schilling was ready to start. He had decided to make sure he lost at least eight out of ten bets but that at the end of each month he was exactly where he wanted to be. Avoiding large odds, staying with short ones for his wins, appearing like an average punter. He had picked out seven tracks within an easy three hour drive, intending to rotate randomly through them, sometimes betting with one agency, or some, or all. No pattern, no regularity, no tell-tale fingerprint, all cased in five randomly rotating accounts.

Over the following two months the app worked perfectly, being taken up by an ever-increasing group of punters. Schilling still appeared the upright corporate and tax citizen his office demanded him to be. Everything he was doing, although a little unorthodox, was perfectly legal. He took pains to keep it that way, even to the point of paying the correct tax on his winnings. At the track no one noticed or cared, he was just the quiet guy in the stands who turned up every so often. Putting a few dollars through the on course bookmakers helped, never any big wins, just small wins, small losses, looking every bit like the cash strapped punter he was trying to portray. Smooth as silk, no problems, no issues. Two or three years of this then just walk away. Maybe.

Larsen was not so settled. Schilling was used to having more than enough money and could control and moderate his behavior, Larsen wasn't. Financially he'd always lived on the edge. His habits kept him nailed there, owing money to people he really didn't want to owe to for things he didn't want anyone to know about. The only limit to his appetite was his income. Greater income just seeped away on more of the same. Now he simply routed his skimmings straight through to his creditors.

He sighed deeply, rubbing salve into gouges across his chest and abdomen. He'd failed to find that one punter he could mimic, one that was consistently above the line. No discernible patterns nothing he brooded, pulling a few shards of glitter from his thigh, it goes straight in and straight out to theirs and I'm nearly square each week. Just one, I need just one of them to make consistent gains in each day, just one … and he broke off cursing himself a fool.

"One day? One day!?! What sort of idiot am I?" He leant forwards, resetting his tracker. One day isn't enough for any pattern, lucky or bent, it needs more time, more time. I've got months of data, what's happening over that? Almost as quickly as he thought it he saw it. Of all the thousands using the app a small slice were above even for the whole period; a smaller slice far enough above to be earning a good income; and of those a very small number stood out as far ahead each month. Bent, they're bent but smart, noting how anything other than a long term view of their entire betting history would not show a thing.

"Now where are you?" muttering, starting to run back the IP traces. It didn't take him long to find it. Five accounts were being run out of one device. Never simultaneously, never in the same sequence, but in a seemingly random mix up that never saw activity in one account for more than four hours in any one day. Taken as a whole it was crystal clear, always a long way up each month. He dug further into the accounts that linked back to the banks and …

He nearly fell off his chair laughing, head thrown back, tears rolling down his face. "I bloody knew it! Perfect, oh god so perfect! Schilling! Mr. I'm-so-damned-corporately-upright Schilling's scamming the ponies!"

For a second blackmail occupied his mind, good god what he could get, but he thought better of it. Best to keep it in his back pocket, keep it for the day he could really use it, really need it. It didn't matter now how Schilling was doing it, Schilling would never go for anything that wasn't ironclad. Ok, whatever you're getting I'll get more, starting to code a simple piggy-back. Every bet you make I'll make as well. But no pussyfooting around, oh no, once there's enough in the kitty I'll at least double your bets. Easy money in the bank with insurance on top. Larsen could hardly control himself, hardly keep a straight face. Finally he was going to get what he knew he deserved.

Thursday, it always seemed to be a Thursday. Schilling felt ready for anything after the green bars. His evening bus load of green horned unicorns now all sported tiny cobalt blue skull caps of varying widths. The largest one covered the whole head above the ears, the smallest the size of a coffee cup. Schilling smiled, settled back. Another mystery, another piece of weirdness and undoubtedly another profitable opportunity to be pursued.

Naawaina carefully adjusted his jacket in the porch light. He'd never felt totally comfortable squeezing his solid Maori frame into it, but he had an image to project, a reputation to keep. I am after all a businessman, just that my tools of trade are a little different. His paw gently closed around the brass dusters in his pocket. A little different but equally effective.

One of the grubs that had particularly sordid tastes had apparently become too financial in the past few months. And grubs with money became indiscreet and dangerous. 'Send a message, find out what's with the new cash,' he'd been told 'and take his handler with you.' Naawaina glanced sideways at Ilmari beside him, short and stocky in slacks and cardigan. He didn't like the Finn, thought him an amateur who was dipping into the merchandise. One day he would get to pay Ilmari a business call and that would be more pleasure than work.

Ilmari took off his sunglasses, carefully placed them in his back pocket and rang the doorbell. The sound of muffled voices made their way out, a curtain to one side seemed to briefly open and close, but no one answered the door. Ilmari rang the doorbell again. Again no response. Ilmari took his mobile phone out.

"Ten seconds, we know you're at home. Just a little friendly chat, no trouble, but if it's not open shortly you'll need another door." He smiled hesitantly at Naawaina. The Kiwi had a reputation, and he was worried. Hopefully this was all about the mark and not him. A series of soft clicks brought his attention back to the door. It opened fully to reveal a disorganized, if clean, interior. The face peering out had the same look. Ilmari stood aside letting the Kiwi's bulk slide past him into the house.

"Thank you." he intoned to the now ashen face, closing the door with an ominous click. "We'll have that little talk," ushering the figure towards the kitchen "as soon as my associate finishes his tour." Larsen nodded glumly.

The Kiwi replaced the blade in his scabbard and, holding the front door open, watched the child walk out into the night. Dressed and removing the last bonds from his wrists he didn't spare a backwards glance. With a small grunt the Kiwi closed and latched the door. Business, it's all business even though I hate what this grub does. As he entered the kitchen he could see Larsen seated on a stool, Ilmari opposite, leaning forwards. A look inside the fridge liberated a cola and two doughnuts, with which he sat on the edge of the benchtop and gave a short nod to Ilmari.

"Right, let's talk money my friend, what you got and what you owe."

Larsen looked bemused. "Owe? I don't owe anything, I'm ahead."

"Yes, you are. You've never been ahead before, not until three months ago."

"Yeah, well, I'm just getting better you know, a few good breaks — "

"Don't put nobody eight thou ahead! Where you getting it?"

"I'm not owing, you get what I use ahead now, I'm always ahead. So what's the issue?"

"You've gone from two thou a month to forty plus, you're getting richer tastes and you're still just a shit puncher at work. You know what that tells me? It tells me something's going on that we need to know about. So. What is it?"

Larsen spread his arms wide in earnest. "Nothing, I told you, a few good breaks at work and that. I mean, I'm pushing it all your way you know, I mean, you guys have just the hottest damned — "

The Kiwi stood up, glaring at Larsen who immediately shut up and shrank back. Brushing the odd crumb from his lapel he replaced Ilmari on the stool, moving closer to Larsen, just inside arm's reach. He smiled gently.

"What perhaps you do not understand is that we are here for your welfare. In fact, we need to know how you are getting all this extra cash not for ourselves, but to help you."

"Help me? How the hell do you — " The impact from the Kiwi's open-handed slap nearly took Larsen's face off, the rapidly reddening shape of five perfectly formed fingers rising from his cheek. The only thing that distracted him from the titanic ringing in his ears was the shock of the backhanded slap on his other cheek as the Kiwi bought his arm back.

"So now you see," taking the dusters from his pocket, obviously and gently sliding his left hand in to them "that telling us will help your welfare. I am, unfortunately, not a patient man so you will understand if I have to, ah, encourage you."

Larsen started to shake, trying to resist the urge to piss. He shrank back on the stool, finding his arms locked behind him. Ilmari leant closer in to him, close enough for Larsen to smell the coffee and riisipuuro on his breath.

"Ok, ok!" still trying to wriggle back. "Yeah, yeah, I've got money, it's horses you know, I'm making it on the ponies."

The Kiwi stared at him, expressionless. "No one does that well unless they are bent or on the inside, and you don't seem to me to be — ”

“No, no!” shrieked Larsen. “No, I got a system, I got a chump who never loses, never, always ends up ahead, believe me,” twisting to look into Ilmari’s eyes “it’s true, believe me!”

Larsen felt a huge paw grab his jaw, pulling him round to look square into the Kiwi’s face. He scrunched his eyes hard, waiting for the hit that would surely take out his teeth. When it didn’t come he gingerly opened one eye.

“You see” noses nearly touching “how talking to us helps you.” Larsen nodded as best he could in that vice-like grip. “So let us continue our conversation, and nice and clear and slow so we have no need to, ah, encourage you further yes?”

“Yes, yes.” he squawked.

“Very well,” leaning back and releasing Larsen “please start again from the beginning. You said ponies yes?”

“Yeah, horse races, ponies. Look, a few months ago … ”

Across town Schilling was attending a different exclusive gathering. For the tenth year in a row corporate profits had outstripped records, congratulations and expensive red flowing like water on the rooftop penthouse. The thirty-eighth floor garden was an extravagant expression of wealth and power, one fitting the head of Schilling’s firm. Schilling smiled to himself. Just one level away from the boardroom and it just doesn’t matter, I could buy this penthouse, the whole block of them, the firm itself. Seeing the managing director across the grass he smiled broadly and raised his glass in salute. Perhaps, just perhaps I have set my sights too low. Unlimited wealth, totally legal, I can with care do nearly anything. He grinned. Yes, another mouthful of red later, anything or anyone.

Across the rooftop the junior levels were getting rowdier. Part of the fun of these events was watching it unfold, watching the flow of high spirits and expensive drink collapse barriers and controls until, at the right point, they could be plucked off one by one for some ‘intensive mentoring’. Part of the game, part of the fringe benefits of power and wanting to gain power. He was happy that Chalker wasn’t here this year, she always played that game harder and keener than he.

The juniors had now moved closer to the glass railing, Schilling looking on bemused as one of the blue skull caps shimmered and then started to shrink at an alarming rate. It's owner, perched precariously on the glass railing giggled, jumped up and started tightrope walking along the ledge. Her blue skull cap rippled, contracted and then popped out of existence. Her heels slipped and soundlessly she plummeted over the edge. Schilling rushed to the railing looking at the crowd of people and cars gathering around the small red dot thirty-eight floors below.

The Kiwi listened attentively to his mobile phone. He had heard Larsen's tale twice and, as improbable as it had sounded, believed him. That Larsen had produced the device and his bank account records after some gentle persuasion had helped. Although he had the answers he was sent to get, there were times you needed to take things upstairs. This was one of them, so he had rung in and now had just finished repeating the story.

On the other end of the line his boss was thinking fast. This one little pervert had, somehow, managed to finger each and every rigged race in the past few months. The fact that somewhere someone else knew meant eventually others would and this little earner would fall, maybe the whole edifice with it. It was too much to risk.

"And he's wiped out his skimming and tracking apps?"

"Yes."

"You have all the software, computer drive, backups?"

"In my bag and in the car."

"And that name again?"

"Schilling."

The Kiwi heard again the short intake of breath.

"Ok. It needs to be wrapped up, cleaned. Erase it. One other thing."

"Yes?"

"Clean up that shit Finn too. No lose ends."

The Kiwi put the mobile pack in his pocket, moving into the kitchen.

"All good?" Ilmari asked.

"Yes." standing behind Ilmari, facing Larsen.

Larsen didn't feel good, the two of them looking at him.

"I'm going to be fine?" looking at Ilmari and the Kiwi in turn.

The Kiwi smiled, grabbed Ilmari's chin in one hand and, placing an arm around his shoulders, gave one rapid pull. Accompanied by the sickening crack of vertebrae Ilmari slumped lifeless to the floor.

Larsen shrank back, mouthing soundlessly as the Kiwi closed the short gap between them.

"Understand," lifting Larsen up from the stool by the neck "this is purely business although I am not particularly fond of you." The knife seemingly appeared by magic in his right hand and, with one stroke, lanced into Larsen's brain through his left eye. Dropping the body to the floor he extracted the knife, wiping it clean on Ilmari's slacks before replacing it in its scabbard. Driving away he saw the first fingers of flame jumping from the front windows.

Friday afternoon Schilling stood on the curb waiting for Chalker. Lost in thought he didn't notice the cab stop or the large presence behind him until something cold, hard and menacing prodded him in the back.

"Eyes front, keep quiet and get into the cab." the presence ordered. Schilling didn't need to see it to know not to argue, so he climbed in through the opened door. The driver stared back impassively through the grille to the man-mountain now sitting next to him, and then took the cab out into the flow of traffic.

Schilling looked beside him. "If it's money you want, I can give it to you, all of it, there's no need — " stopping cold at the look coming his way.

"I asked you to be quiet Mr. Schilling," the Kiwi hissed "so please remain so. Your money is nothing."

Schilling sighed, looked ahead. If it's not money I'm a hostage then, and in real trouble. The cab continued it's journey in silence.

Schilling came to, bound to a chair in a small, bare room. Faint shadows danced in time with the sway of a solitary bulb. He didn't know how long he had been out but he knew how he had gotten that way. His glasses lay broken on the floor, the taste of blood in his mouth. Chin on bare chest he could see small welts and bruises, too small for the pain that placing them had given. Grudgingly he admitted that the man-mountain knew his stuff, applied the right lever to the right place. And now he – or they – knew everything.

He lifted his face to the mirrored wall opposite. He looked a mess, blue skull cap and green bar notwithstanding. At least they left my underwear on, spared one final indignity.

The Kiwi delicately wiped the last few spots of blood from his knuckles. For the second time in a week he had heard an unlikely, impossible, explanation of events. And for the second time he knew beyond a doubt the explanation was true. Rods. Rods on horses. He shook his head. Discarding the tissue he buttoned his jacket.

Schilling was starting to regain his senses, his composure. He had no illusions about his situation, precarious no matter what the outcome. But he had the skill, the capability no one had, a bargaining chip. It was simply another business dealing he told himself, one with different rules and roles, but business none the less.

The Kiwi waited in silence. The immaculate, slightly built figure standing at the one-way mirror was, since his mother's death, the only person that held his total and unquestioning respect and obedience. They combined an iron will and professional self-control with clinically cold and calculatingly rational cruelty. That they controlled a legal conglomerate acting as a front for the largest illegal operation in the country wasn't surprising. That in this, the most male of male dominated arenas she was a woman, was.

She turned back from the glass towards the Kiwi. "Let this be another lesson for you," Chalker started "in this business anything can happen. This man has helped us before but now … " She sighed gently. Really, what did she care that Schilling made some extra out of the horses, but his stupidity with Larsen was unforgivable. And more so using ReoProm as the vehicle, placing her in the spotlight.

"Business is business, never forget that." She turned her back to him, moving towards the exit. "I want you to … "

Schilling jumped instinctively as the door opened and the Kiwi lumbered in. He felt his stomach knot and cold sweat break out on his forehead. Not from the Kiwi, not for the same impassive cold look on his eyes. But next to him, on the mirrored wall, he could see his own reflection. And on the top of his head his blue skull cap rippled, contracted, then popped out of existence.

WEATHERMAN

I like the cold. In fact, I have a real physical need to feel the cold, to be in bed wrapped tightly against the outside, bare feet searching for the cold corners while my nose sticks out like some polar crocodile. I enjoy walking through snow, feeling my face sting from rain that's nearing hail and having the wind rub my ears to beetroot red. Which is a pity really, seeing how I live here in tropical Queensland, the temperature hardly falling below twenty degrees Celsius all year and three hundred odd days out of each year being without rain.

It's all put up out of deference to Angelique. She can't stand the cold or rain and who, having the money in the family while I was still working my way up the academic ladder, had the major say in where we settled. Not that we don't compromise. I get two weeks holiday at the height of the Australian summer anywhere in the world, which usually means the northern hemisphere in the deep of winter (last year it was Reykjavik, a place I can appreciate). Angel suffers patiently through it all until we take the other two weeks anywhere she wants it. In fact it had all worked marvelously well until that year when the faculty just couldn't do without the services of this particular climatologist, and I had to suffer through one of the worst summers on record.

One evening about two and a half weeks into what should have been our holiday I was with Angel on our verandah wondering what I had done to deserve this. Shirtless, with rivulets of sweat pouring down my back and chest, I lay sprawled across a swing chair sucking savagely on a rapidly diminishing ice cube. I had not been able to eat all day for the heat, and to add insult to injury the faculty had decided at the last minute they really didn't need me after all. Pity they didn't make that discovery when tickets out of the place were still available. Not in the best of moods I saw that Angel was enjoying the heat, balanced daintily on the edge of the chair not a hair out of place, not even the smallest signs of perspiration visible. Needless to say her very audacity at being so comfortable needled me no end.

I hauled myself up on one elbow. "It's not fair. I should be rigid with frostbite right now." Energy totally expended I sank back down.

Angel regarded me as you would a five year old brat. I could be petulant and irritating at times, and I had just about used my annual quota of both that day. Thankfully she was feeling conciliatory and not combative.

"Well for somebody who claims to know so much about the weather you're not doing too much about it. I thought that a smart guy like you would find a way to make it more bearable." she crooned, stroking my hair and creating a small Niagara that cascaded over my nose onto the floor. With a passing chuckle at the look on my face she moved back inside. I didn't give it much of a second thought, thinking she was only sparring with me as we do.

Looking back now I can't help but think she was more than half serious. I also can't help but wish like hell she'd never opened her mouth.

Of course next month we had forgotten all about it. Angel was busy with her trading and I was buried in my office (really just a corner of the tech lab) getting the latest results from my micro climate simulation project. The simulations were bringing the right numbers out so I was feeling ok. All I had to do was wait until the next fifty million dollar research grant came around (fat chance) and I could try to really get that part of the Dandenongs warmed up. What I was in reality left with was theory, a bit of prediction, and more and more modelling.

It was then that Pradesh came bursting through the door. I sprang up just in time to arrest the hurtling student in mid stumble, plonking him bodily into my vacated chair.

"Pradesh what's the matter? What's happened?" I assumed that some piece of bad news had wound him up so. He didn't respond, just continued to draw deep breaths, but his eyes darted between mine and a handful of crumpled pages he was holding on to as life itself.

"Look at this! Can we really do it?"

My heart sank. Probably another red herring or Government statement about increasing funding that once again nobody had bothered to make sure was right. I liked Pradesh so I decided to at least feign interest. I took the papers from him and flattened them against the desktop.

I had read barely a paragraph when my stomach started to tighten up. By the time I had finished the last page I could feel something stirring inside me. I looked him in the eye.

"Where did you get this? When did it come in?"

"Just now on the fax. I was standing there sending one out and this dropped in. I couldn't believe it – are we going to go for it or what?"

I just smiled. In my hand I had a genuine NASA request asking me to form a team, spend one hundred million dollars of their end of year appropriation and reduce flood risk in the sub-continent. Was I or what? My smile turned into a fully-fledged inane grin. "Fancy a trip to the States?"

Things happened fast. Pradesh, myself, and my other grad student Kate would meet two of my ex-students at CalTech to form the core of the team. Facilities, mainframe time, accommodation, everything was being supplied outside the appropriation so we had no problems there, and to say that the Yanks were welcoming would be putting it mildly. Before we had even finalized the team details we felt as if we were part of the family. But there was one problem. A hundred million sounds like mega bucks when you're struggling on forty thousand dollar research grants, but to do what I had in mind properly would take a fair bit more. Although the technique I had in mind would be a sure fire success I knew we could barely just get to the mid-point with the budget we had.

I had told Angel at the start about the whole deal. As time came nearer for the off she noticed my mood becoming more and more somber. It was one cool afternoon as autumn was about to make way for winter that she confronted me. Sitting beachside with our toes in the sand we were talking about nothing in particular when she started.

"Okay, out with it." she said turning to face me across a Bacardi and Coke. "You should be the happiest damned man on the planet but you've been moping around as if you expected the end of the world. I'm not sure what's going on but I think we should talk."

I pulled my eyes from her thighs and sighed. "Yeah, you'd think I'd be leading the conga line wouldn't you. I dunno if I'm sounding ungrateful but I'm not sure if it's going to be enough."

"What?"

"The money for the project." I leant forward a bit. "I've had something in mind for the past few years that I thought I could never do, something I know can work brilliantly, and when this came in I thought I had the budget to swing it. But I've done the figures and it is just not enough. Another fifty and I could just about with some begging, but another hundred and I could do it with style."

"It's really short? I mean, there are no corners you could cut, no alternatives, no options?"

I laughed. "What do you think I've been doing at night for the past month? I've been over everything, all the options, all the alternatives. If I can do this and do it the way I want it will make everything I've done before seem like a spit into a strong breeze."

"You've never quite told me what it was. You've dropped some pretty obtuse hints but ..."

"Ok," I admitted "I've been secretive. But here it is for

what it's worth, and when I'm finished you'll see why I can't do it. For starters ..."

It took me the best part of three hours during which she never once said anything. Once I was finished we sat in silence for an hour. I could see that she was deep in thought. She finally spoke sometime after the sun had left.

"I've never known you to lie or exaggerate but I thought you'd just started. But I see what you mean and I think I understand it. Tell me, the extra, what currency?"

"I haven't thought about it to be honest."

She sighed. "Where would you do your shopping?"

"The States, possibly Europe, more than likely France or Germany."

"And how much can you access now?"

I had to think hard. "Well the last time I looked I had about fifty-three and another forty-six in the States once we start."

"Can you draw on it?"

"Yeah."

"Do you trust me?"

I looked at her strangely. "Of course." And then I knew. "How much do you want?"

She drew some figures in the sand. "Forty-six I'll need for three days but I need you to do something specific with the other seven. And I need you to do exactly what I say exactly when I say. If you do, we can make this fly. If you don't, well ..."

The following day a rather large bank draft was drawn up and I sent Pradesh and Kate to set up shop in the States with sixty thousand. I promised to join them in a week or so, and let them off at the airport. As I pulled out my mobile went off.

"Hon, Angel. It's time. Be at McLellands in twenty minutes to start."

"Ok."

"Right, let's go over it again. Go in at exactly two o'clock and ..." she continued giving precise instructions and having me repeat them verbatim.

"Clear?"

I had nearly run off the road twice writing it down. "No probs. See you later."

We did private business we wanted quiet and discrete through McLellands, a (barely) reputable company that charged more but said less than other brokers. McLelland was happy to see me but I suspect happier to see the bank draft. After the two o'clock transaction he thought I had gone for good, but come three was surprised to see me back on his doorstep. The additional commission helped ease his pain over my return but he looked nonplussed as I sat down again at ten to five.

"Again? Haven't you had enough? Do you know what happened ten minutes after you left, you coulda screwed it to the wall if you had just left it sitting instead of diving off. If you want back in well mate that horse has bolted."

I eyed him cautiously and slipped a tab of paper to him. "No, I just want to dump it for this. What's the rate now?"

He told me, and I told him to put the offer at eighty-five percent value. His jaw dropped. Before he could speak, I cut in.

"Don't ask, I've got my reasons. If you need an explanation you can put your rate up two percent but just do it now."

His jaw went back where it belonged. I had touched him at heart, he had always been easy to buy. His hands went up. "Ok, whatever you say, no questions asked."

He left the room muttering something about the mental defects of bloody greenie academics and came back in at ten past five with a check and an evil grin.

"Well you probably take the prize. I've done what you said and after all that stuffing around you're down by three and a half. I hope you have a nice day, thanks for the commission."

I left with check in hand. The closer I came to home the deeper my gloom became. I had lost three and a half out of seven but I took some solace as I knew Angel was probably making that up and more. The hours at home dragged on and I ended up glued in front of late night TV. The exchange market news nearly broke my heart, all the movements indicating I had missed my chance. Me and Johnny Walker got to know each other better.

I had been drunk, sobered up and drunk again by the time Angel came home. I was feeling pretty dirty but I said nothing as she sat down. I felt that instead of flying this little puppy was all over and done with. Maybe exile to Siberia wouldn't be that bad.

Angel put her head on my shoulder and let out a long sigh. "I guess you think I am some sort of moron or something. You've seen the rates I suppose?"

"Yeah. But I still love you."

"That's nice to know, but don't give up on me quite yet. Do you know why I asked you to lose that money? You do know that I actually wanted you to lose it, don't you?"

"Can't say that I did or do, you know. It'd be the first time you set out to make a loss if it was."

"Well I couldn't be the one to kick the first domino."

She reached into her briefcase. "But I had to be there to make sure the rest went. I had to hang on for a while to make it happen and I'm not going to try and explain as you don't understand cross rates or hedging no matter how hard I try. Put it simply that a smart trader knows how to play one off against another. And, darling, you know I'm the best."

She had slid a small square of paper into my lap while she was speaking. I looked down and saw a US currency draft for three hundred and fifty million dollars.

"That enough?" She laughed.

Enough? I nearly wet myself.

My departure from Australia was made in high spirits, Angel adding to it by riding on the back of the research money with some of our own. I had doubts about what the NASA Grants Board would say, but was pleasantly surprised with their reaction at our first meeting. I had just started my 'Oh, by the way I have an extra couple of hundred million' speech and was wondering if it would be believed when the Board Director came up to me.

"Fantastic!" she exclaimed, grabbing me in an ebullient bear hug. "And they say the spirit of free enterprise doesn't live down under!" And that was that.

The team knew better than to ask questions and in any case were too far into their work to have the time. Pradesh had managed to locate and identify the materials we required and Kate was molding the rest of the team into shape on the design and device build. I busied myself spending until it hurt and watching it all go together. Even working feverishly with and all the assistance we had it was still a hard slog to completion. Finally, eight months later, we found ourselves in the Florida dawn watching the crawler transporter carry our precious load to the launch pad. We had a window, we had a deadline, and we had beaten it by a sliver over twenty four hours. And we had twenty two million dollars change.

The launch was flawless and we assembled at JPL two days later to watch the devices' construction, the drones already having deployed in orbit. The day consisted of nothing more than watching the automated construction of our device which after eighteen hours resembled exactly what it should – a large, appreciably convex saucer some three kilometers in diameter. A central column four hundred meters high protruded sunwards from its center. The surface of the saucer consisted of myriad small, mirrored shutter like panes built around radial spokes. The end of each spoke was connected by nanotube to the top of the column and likewise to a lesser protrusion on the Earthwards side. At the moment all the shutters were aligned so that they were edge on to both Sun and Earth.

"Always the way it is, another simple, elegant solution." Kate mused.

I smiled. Elegant yes, simple not quite so. It was the first question I had put to Kate when she applied for the Doctoral program, and her answer was the reason I had taken her into my circle of students. 'How do you heat up one square kilometer of ocean?' which usually elicited the same series of hydro-thermal, bore hole options. Kate had suggested what I myself thought. Take a small mirror. Stick it in orbit and presto, ocean heated. With the device however a simple command would turn it either into a lens or a reflector by angling the mirrors. In the neutral state the device was, for all intents and purposes, transparent. I laughed.

"Not the way you see it?" she asked.

"Oh no," I offered "it's not that. I'm just wondering what Orville and Wilbur Wright would think of what we've done with their wing warping."

"Somehow I think they'd approve."

Months later back at the University I was still monitoring the device. The preliminary data were encouraging, if anything better than projected. It seemed a success. Even with a further twelve months for the impact on weather patterns to be felt everything pointed to our goals being met. All we had to do was monitor it as the automated routine continued.

A year and a half down the track and life rolled on as usual. Pradesh and Kate had both graduated. Angel and I were now ridiculously well off and had solid plans to retire by forty-five to open a café bookshop. The device was working as expected, it's monitoring now being automated out of JPL leaving me with a tenuous link via the stream of research papers I was publishing.

Angel and I were sitting on the same verandah in the same place as we were when the whole episode started, watching a mid-summer pastel sunset.

"Strange," she started "the days aren't quite as harsh as I remember them."

"How do you mean, harsh?"

"Well, it seems as if the edge has gone off the days. It's not quite as hot and I'm positive that it's less humid than it has been."

I chuckled quietly to myself. "What were we doing not more than three years ago?"

She creased her brows slightly. "Not much, you hadn't started the project then and we were stuck here. In fact," she continued with more than a touch of sarcasm "the only thing

I remember clearly is a constant whining."

I leant back and put my arm around her. "I recall that you asked why I didn't have the brains to sort out the summer heat while I lay here sweating to death."

"Did I?"

"Oh yes, and I didn't forget. In fact, I have done something about it."

Angel stared at me, eyes narrowed. "What exactly do you mean?"

"Well, the device doesn't have to work all the time on the main project, it has a big down time up there and because of its positioning it can work on a third lesser known weather node in the region." I smiled broadly, looking her in the eyes.

"So, I have added just a couple of lines to the programming and it's going to chop off about two degrees from our summer maximums."

Angels' eyes widened slightly, but then retreated to slits. "They'll find out what you've done eventually you realize, don't you?"

"Nah, they won't," I countered derisively "it only has to do this for another two months and the pattern's changed forever. I can then just wipe the lines and then that's that. No ones the wiser and this place is then just that little more civilized."

"Hmmmmm," was her only comment as she settled back "I certainly hope so."

Three things happened in quick succession that neatly destroyed my carefully laid plans. Firstly a minor meteor shower took out the communications antenna on the device leaving it still functioning but unable to talk to us or we to it. Secondly the US Congress took a sharp axe to all expenditure. Near the top of the list was NASA; and on the top of NASA's list was JPL; and on the top of JPL's was the monitoring of the device.

Finally all the over work, late nights, bad eating habits and stress hit me. I don't know if it's possible to have a minor nervous breakdown, but if there is then what I got sure as hell wasn't. I quit my faculty job, retired at forty-two instead of forty-five. I couldn't do much more than dress and clean myself for the next eighteen months. Worse yet as part of it I totally lost track of my work, a common defense mechanism I am told.

The upshot? The device was forgotten totally, erased from the minds of NASA and myself and left to get on with its programming uninterrupted.

Retirement has treated Angel and myself well. Our café bookshop pays its own way, and is relatively stress free. With both of us retired we have time enough for ourselves, and that's what really matters. And my legacy still continues. Monsoon is now much gentler, predictable and still replenishes the lands and river deltas. El Nino and La Nina continue in a much lessened way, severe drought and flood being relegated to history. The device continued on its merry way for another ten years before failing totally, more than enough time to produce a permanent change in weather patterns.

And of my other special project?

Well, I like the cold. In fact, I have a real physical need to feel the cold, to be in bed wrapped tightly against the outside, bare feet searching for the cold corners while my nose sticks out like some polar crocodile. I enjoy walking through snow, feeling my face sting from rain that's nearing hail and having the wind rub my ears to beetroot red. Which is fortunate, seeing how I live here in hemi boreal Queensland, the temperature hardly struggling above eight degrees Celsius and rain two hundred and fifty odd days out of each year. But Angel ...

MY BROTHERS KEEPER

It had been one of those years that just seemed to get worse and worse I reflected as the shuttle docked two hundred kilometers above the Pacific ocean. Yet it had all started so damned well. I had finally managed to get a posting into the United Nations landing a highly paid and yet truly irrelevant position as chief negotiator in the extra-terrestrial department. What a joke that had been I thought morosely as I sat in zero gee trying to close my briefcase, a position with all the respect, money and influence of Senior Section head yet with absolutely no possibility of having to actually perform the function entrusted to it. Yeah sure, there were plans and committees, round table discussions and contingency plans, but all of it carried on much in the fashion as the builders of the Titanic regarded icebergs.

Then it turned August. I will never forget that day, looking out of my office fifty floors above New York watching a monstrous spacecraft sliding slowly over the Bay with, I was to learn later, a dozen or more doing the same thing in all the major capitals of the world. And then the damned broadcast. I could hardly stop my hands trembling when I glanced at the transcript I had held on the entire flight. My eyes kept being drawn to the page although I knew word for word, as fresh and disturbing as that first day.

'Humanity,' it began and that voice seemed to jump out of

my mind again 'you have existed long enough to warrant the privileges and responsibilities afforded to custodians of great things. Yet you have consistently proven yourselves abject failures, creatures ruled more by whim than principle. It has been decided that, as a race that has shown itself incapable of controlling itself, never mind what is entrusted to it, you will be directed by the council in all future matters. Accordingly you will stop all forms of manufacturing and industrial processing; to cease all activities, including transportation, that produce air, water or land pollution; universally adopt birth control measures; lay down and deactivate all weapons and weapons systems; and to entrust to your United Nations all functions of government of your nations so they may implement the directives of the Council. You have thirty days, after which we will return to this spot to transport a representative from your United Nations to our vessel for further instructions.'

With that the panic and grandstanding had set in. I remembered the disbelief, then the outrage; the Chinese attempt to nuke the ship that appeared over Beijing, and the resultant total destruction of that city; Russian claims and US counter claims; and in the end despondency when nothing could be done but accept what had been put to us. Even in that month a new distribution of food worldwide and reversion to older methods of transport had started, and at least ten million people had died as third world nations strove to take what the first world had before that too was cut off.

I thought that it would be a job for the big boys, a job not entrusted to me, but I forgot that I was the only player in town. So here I was, airsick and scared witless, struggling to follow a vaguely female humanoid into an alien spacecraft. Thankfully I had brought my pills and they had turned gravity back on again.

Coming out of what I assumed was the docking bay, I was led along a narrow passageway that seemed to be lit from every point, but then at the same time from no point at all. My guide seemed quite amused by my looks, particularly when I asked her about it.

"Frankly human, I despair of your questions. Even a child knows that the light senses your presence and rushes to meet it."

Finally we came to a non-descript room with a single large chair situated in the center, facing a large tank that occupied two sides from floor to ceiling, seeming infinitely deep.

"I will return when you are finished with the others." my guide commented as she sat me in the chair. "I would dearly love to see your reaction to this, but apparently they have some private matters to discuss with you." With that she moved out of the room, leaving me alone with the empty tank.

I peered deeper into the tank and out of the far reaches, beyond where the feeble light of the room penetrated, three large shapes moved slowly towards me. Marine life obviously I thought, alien marine life. As the three shapes moved closer my heart leapt into my mouth and I began to shake. What was in front of me was a pair of dolphins, accompanied by a pilot whale, the burning light of intelligence clearly in their eyes. I sank back into the chair as far as I could, trying to move between the folds of cushion.

"About time we had one of you cornered," a voice boomed inside my head "and you had better listen carefully." I knew that I was being addressed by the pilot whale, but how?

"Telepathy four limbs, telepathy. Although I can't quite remember if your sub species has any of that rudimentary faculty left. And yes, it is me the pilot whale talking, and yes I can hear your thoughts. If it makes you any easier, you can speak normally. It makes no difference to me."

Christ, I thought, what's going on? What do fish have to do with anything?

"Not fish," the first dolphin thought "but two related sea species, what you call whales and dolphins. And as to what we have to do with it, well, quite frankly, we instigated this and are now the ruling body of the planet."

I reached into my jacket pocket with shaking hands and, after tearing the cap off with my teeth, popped four valium into my mouth.

"It won't help you know. Our communication with you is through the subconscious link, so it just makes it easier for us. Thanks anyway, we can get this over with quicker. Things to do, places to go you know."

"Stop this crap!" I screamed as I leapt from the chair. Obviously valium was no help. Perhaps I should switch to mogadon or heroin. "You're fish. You swim in the sea, get caught in nets, end up on plates with chips and peas and perform tricks at Sea World. You sit, no float there and try to tell me that you now rule Earth through some Council that sits god knows where? Come on, you," directed at the pilot whale "can't even outrun a bloody harpoon or hide from Norwegian 'science' boats and you'll have me believe this? And the only intelligence that you lot give is the ability or ring bells for fish and act in D grade TV shows. I must be mad!"

"No, unfortunately for you you're not, although we could make you if you wish. Like this," with which I was no longer standing with my nose against the glass, but floating two feet in front of the whale in the tank "or this," and I was lying on the deck of a Japanese whaler being slit end from end as I struggled to regain the sea "or even this." and I was moving through the abattoirs with the rest of my herd as someone grabbed me and placed a knife to my throat. "But we don't want you like that." I was back in the relative safety of the chair, being sick all over the floor.

As I regained what was left of my composure I realized that this was for real, and so were they. If anything was to be salvaged out of this, I had better cooperate and learn.

"That' s better, now we can communicate, one intelligent race to a nearly intelligent one."

"Fine, but how did you get like this? I mean, we had no idea that you were intelligent to this degree. After all, you have no artefacts, no visible science, no buildings, no — "

I was cut off in mid-sentence by the second dolphin. "One of your race's basic mistakes I'm afraid. A conviction that intelligence and material possessions are necessarily connected. Not true dear boy, not true at all. You must understand that we have been evolving and developing as a species for longer than you have, developing further and faster. We once cooperated with one of your branch species many centuries ago, but they left once they realized your particular variant would be numerically superior. They didn't want a part of it, didn't even want you finding their artefacts in case you found them."

"We had the chance" continued the pilot whale "to go with them, but we decided not to as we thought your race and ours may learn together and grow. We held out great hope for you as a species, and still do, although our disappointment is great."

"What about our fishing and whaling fleets? Surely you can't have me believe that you let us slaughter you just because you thought we had hope?"

"No, not at all. Our group conscience is not tied to an individual, but to the species as a whole. An individual is simply the mechanism that acts, in part, to sustain the group. All thought, experience and discovery is shared by and, more importantly is preserved in the group."

"Think about it," the second continued "we like you are carnivores. How could we eat other sentient beings, or be eaten, if we were individual consciousness? It would be the highest crime, something that still makes your species repulsive, your wanton destruction of sentience. It is a fact of life that things must be eaten. Hence, we did not object to this if it was to sustain your species, as we lost nothing. We do much the same ourselves with those we feed on, except we choose the oldest and weakest, ensuring continuation of the species. Our former environment was finely tuned along these lines."

"Your consumption of us" the plot whale now agitated "was no threat to our common consciousness unless reduced below our critical mass which happened — "

"You're extinct!" I had finally remembered why I was so shocked at seeing it. All those WWF reports had sunk in.

"Not quite. Once it became critical we simply moved wholesale under the Arctic ice pack and evaded you. From which point we simply left the planet, came here, and have done quite nicely for ourselves. You see, space travel is really simple once you have certain premises established. We had the ability about seven thousand years ago but saw no need to use it, that is until the troubles. Strange species," directed to the others "trying so hard for something when the very methods ensure failure."

"We wanted nothing more than to be left alone to our thoughts, research and pleasure. But even this you denied us. For two hundred years now you have continually poisoned and destabilized our home habitat to the point where we can perhaps never return. In fact, you are so short sighted that you cannot appreciate that it also threatens your existence."

"So," thinking I had the plot "you decide to establish control over Earth and rehabilitate it so that the major species can coexist?" Not a bad plan really, these guys seemed to have it figured out and a world without smog would be quite pleasant.

"Well yes and no." They seemed to be taking some delight in this, and it made me uneasy. "You see, we have little real control, but they do listen closely to us. In that we wish to restore the planet to its original state well yes, that's true. We also want your species to be made aware of our presence, and that of the other four sentient and intelligent species that have been putting up with you for the past millennia. As far as coexistence goes, well, we found a better place that is not ruined by land based life so we have shifting there permanently. Your species on the other hand is deemed too dangerous to be allowed off the planet's surface. By getting rid of your industry, we not only fulfil our altruistic notions of equity, but also keep you from doing to the galaxy what you did to Earth."

I sat back thinking, full of despair. Sure we had acted out of ignorance, but such a sentence. What had they thought? That without industry we'd be stuck there? If they'd done it without ... I shut my mind off, blanketing the thought harshly. "So we're to be quarantined?"

"Correct. And permanently. There is nothing left to

discuss. You know what is required, and you will receive detailed instructions later. Just do what you are told." With which the three shapes left.

Taken back to the shuttle I knew what was to be done. In a new society without machinery, starvation or war time enough for thought would exist. If they had done it without obvious technology, then we could too. Perhaps it would take longer, but we would get there. But this time not as colonists or conquerors. No, this time we would travel and explore for knowledge, not gain. Hopefully.

As the shuttle left on its homeward journey three shapes floated effortlessly in the void, the need for shadow play of normalcy removed. Looking into the vessel without looking, they moved into the synapses and connections of one being's mind subtly changing it. The exterior remained the same, as did the functions, but the core was enhanced. For this emissary could now link to others, not that he would know it for no other of his species could. But his children, and all generations from there could, the basis for real human development being laid.

Their task done, they moved with their fellows to their new home and settled into life for life's sake.

And waited for their ancient companions to join them.

TIME IN LIEU

Erica was impressed. "Three weeks? Three whole weeks! How'd you get that approved?"

"It was easy, I've been saving for two years so I'm owed." Janice leant closer. The tea room was less crowded than usual but still the hubbub of voices made normal conversation difficult. "I've also got some time in lieu so I just made a little song and dance and hey presto, three weeks leave."

"I can't imagine it! What are you going to do with yourself?"

'Oh I've an idea, something a bit different."

"Your suite, I hope it is to your tastes." The steward held Janice's bag as she stepped into the room. Circular, barely four meters across the floor, curved walls and domed ceiling were all a uniform dull grey. Dominated by a double bed and recliner on what looked like a Persian rug, a small bedside table and lamp completed the furnishings. She went to the chair, sinking into the soft enfolding leather and smiled.

"It's beautiful, I can't believe all this is just for me."

"Thank you ma'am. They are all period pieces, the rug a twentieth century antique. If I could just demonstrate how the services are controlled … "

"They leave weekly so it does fit your plans." The travel

agent was all smiles, as well they should be given the cost Janice thought. "I'm quite excited for you, I don't believe we've ever had one of these."

"I've been planning this for years." She squirmed, spreading her elbows to eke out a little more personal space. "You can book it for me today?"

"Of course! I just need some details … "

"… plus voice activation." The clip of the steward's heels rang from the steel plate as he placed the control down on the bedside table. Not for him to walk on the rug, that would never do, it was the guest's privilege.

"It seems simple enough. Could you just go through the menu options again? I'd hate to be stuck on stir fry or foie gras the whole time."

"Of course ma'am," beaming at being able to display his knowledge again "if you would care to press the yellow … "

"The *Polaris*, the luxury I can understand, but she's doing this!" Erica slid the flimsy across to Deidre.

"Seriously? You just never know, you think you know someone then they go and do something like this."

"I know, it's so perverted isn't it?"

"Utterly anti-social."

"I wouldn't have believed it if I hadn't seen it."

The wall closed behind the retreating steward, sealing Janice in. She took off her clothes, picking up the thick bathrobe before sending the closet back into the floor. She hesitated, thinking better of it. Hell, she'd signed up for this and her nakedness was symbolic really. She allowed herself a small giggle as she threw the bathrobe on the chair.

The first meal on the *Polaris* told her where she was. Silver cutlery, gold trimmed china and crystal glasses were light years from tube paste food and crowded benches. She'd felt at ease rapidly, everyone else assumed a certain level of social standing simply by being here. It never crossed anyone's mind she was just ordinary.

"My dear, how exciting!" gushed Doctor Martens. "It is something I've never heard of, how could they have this and not actually let on?"

"It's not advertised," Janice said "practically no call for it I'm told."

"Well, I have no doubts." Mrs. Martens interjected "I don't think there would be, I mean, how on earth could one expose oneself like that?"

"Oh I don't know dearest, it would be quite the experience I think." he replied.

"But all by ones' self? My dear" taking Janice's hand in hers "what a brave, brave soul you are."

She filled the bowl to the brim with hot soapy water, an exorbitant luxury. She'd toyed with the idea of a shower but no, waiting would make it so much sweeter. She dunked her face again, blowing bubbles and trying to laugh at the same time. Drying her face she sent towel and bath fitting back.

The dull grey room now changed to pale orange. Janice looked about in anticipation, five minutes left. She lay on the recliner wrapped in the absolute silence, tilting back until she was gazing up at the domed roof.

"It's a real possibility in our profession, so we all do it, although only for a day and not in the same luxurious surroundings." Captain Ström continued over dinner. "Some see it as one of the little perks of the job, others more as a test of endurance."

Janice smiled, enjoying her last meal on the *Polaris*. One day out, they would part ways in a few hours to be reunited sixteen days later. "I can understand, it's hard to explain how I feel. Excited, nervous, maybe a little scared."

"Exactly how I felt. Believe me it's lifechanging, transformative. It's not lightly done, and you by choice." He raised his glass. "A toast to your courage and openness."

The room changed from pale orange to soft blue, lights

fading, the signal. Janice was truly by herself, the *Polaris* many lightyears away. Involuntarily she gripped the arms of her chair, tensing but then slowly relaxing, talking to herself. It's what you planned for, the scrimping, saving, stupidly long working hours, all for this, for the fear and trepidation of this moment and those beyond, for the stupendous solitary silence. Even so a lifetime of being no more than two meters from another human being, living cheek to jowl to sweat stained stinking body with thirty billion other people left an indelible, vociferous other inside her. Her heart and soul knew she was the only person within five hundred lightyears, cocooned alone in her pale blue goldfish bowl. It was only her mind that needed convincing.

The floor became transparent, leaving her on a magic carpet suspended in inky darkness strewn with thousands of points of light, russet pink nebulae bursting through darkened gas lanes searching for nearby yellow suns. She imagined herself in some enormous snow-globe, eternity behind her, blue shielded roof above. Breathtaking in scale, heart rendingly empty yet full, a soft-spoken command and the furnishings vanished leaving her floating naked to the cosmos.

"Not quite, it is something more, quite more." Captain Ström had the pleasure of Mrs. Martens' company on the bridge, watching the small dot recede rapidly on the *Polaris'* tracking screen.

"I'm not sure I could, I get all overwrought if I'm by myself in an elevator never mind out there. To each their own, I hope she enjoys it."

Captain Ström gazed wistfully at the tracking screen. "Oh she will indeed Mrs. Martens, she will indeed."

Janice had lost all sense of time. Captured by the stars below she felt herself changed, the walls and roof now fading rapidly until they too were gone. She now seemingly hung unprotected, alone, utterly exposed to and wrapped in the universe.

Her mind rejected what her eyes told her as her heart leapt, rejected it again even as acceptance dawned, realization that the stars strung out as diamonds on velvet behind her were not so in front. She remembered to breathe, short ragged breaths heaving oxygen through her body to eyes transfixed, irises huge dilated black orbs soaking it in, feeding it all to her now ravenous mind and soul.

Directly above the eagle nebula hung gloriously as if waiting to pounce, vaulted buttresses cradling, enfolding her. Soaring towers of interstellar gas surrounded her, burning luminous green, red, indigo blue as millions of young close-packed stars fed their furious growth, a cosmic nursery birthing blue white life, beauty, belonging.

Janice felt the years fall, the layer upon layer of confining communal conformity peel away, the griefs and frustrations of one small life erased and uplifted by the infinite, finding herself as she lost herself. Her tears matched only her laughter, the soundtrack of her rebirth.

SMALL COMFORT

I burst out of the crowded doorway, slipping between jumbled autorickshaws east into three lanes of crawling Chandni Chowk traffic heading west. It's easy enough dodging grasping hands, harder to outpace hurled curses and cries. I jump through roadside crowds, weaving through shoppers and tourists, bouncing off street vendors as I careen down into the maze of back alleys and open shopfronts. A wrong foot and a cloud of red chilli powder explodes behind me, canisters spraying out from the tottering stall; I don't look back, just keep weaving and dodging, heading deeper. Ashkay appears as if by magic on my right as I jink left across a solitary patch of green, thrusting the handbag into his rucksack even as we're running headlong into the Metro square. Finished I fall against the railing, panting laughing as he disappears into the crowded hall. I'm now nothing but your everyday left behind child, ten years of shabbily dressed vagrant on the streets of Delhi. Dirty, ordinary, thin, I'm not the kid with the Gucci handbag now, just one of the countless street urchins sitting in the dust waiting for god knows what god knows when. I hear the plink of five rupees hitting the dirt in front of me, looking up into the condescending eyes of an elderly western tourist. She smiles, tousles my hair and then walks away happy having rescued another of the poverty-stricken masses with the supreme act of sacrifice, almost ten cents american. I pick the coin up giggling after her. She's headed downtown, our main patch today. Maybe I'll see inside the rest of her purse later.

It's the end of a good but long day, resting my legs in front atop the garbage heaped twelve feet up, watching the trains pull in and out along three sets of tracks in front, four storied slums behind. Chai and cardamom mixed with dung and sweat scents the evening air, the constant blaring of car horns, cows and rumbling freight cars for background music. Below me I can see Ashkay with his stupid grin and Sontash trying to start a fire, they're nearly all here sitting in a circle as I go down into the fold between the heaps, tossing two wallets and a handbag into the pile in front of Pradesh. He grunts and looks away, it's the best I'll get out of him but it's enough, he's nearly seventeen and bigger than me, I've done good today and he knows it.

Sontash has the fire going steadily, its glow fighting a losing battle against the city lights. Ashkay pokes me in the ribs, pointing with his bottle. Pradesh's put his shirt down on the ground and starts to pour out the contents of each bag and wallet onto it. He tosses the empties to Sontash who, after checking, throws them on the fire. It doesn't take Pradesh long and soon neat piles of cash, credit cards, passports, IDs, coins, mobile phones and assorted junk stand in front of him. He takes the IDs and passports and puts them by his side. The mobile phones go to Indrani, she sets to work extracting the sim cards, tossing them after the handbags into the fire. Everything else is divided up ten ways, one for each of us and two for him. Like the rest I scrabble getting my cut in my hands, nearly two thousand rupees, less than normal but enough. Stuffing the notes in the front of my pants, my fist closed on a few coins, I jump up and head off down the railway tracks. I don't like hanging around, when it gets late old boys come over and start drinking, then there's the police and if we're unlucky the favors. Ashkay still carries his knife after last time, says he'll cut theirs off if they try again.

I make a quick turn left and dropping my sandals at the

gate head into the temple. It seems peaceful in the early night, the shadows dancing on the pillars softer, gentler as if the candles and lamps burn holier after sunset. I put my coins in the hundi and make my puja to Ganesh; I've always liked Ganesh, strong, good looking, huge belly. One day my belly will be like his, fat on good food, rich food, western food. I rise and the priest dots my head with the tilak before I head back out across the road to eat with Ashkay. Dahl fry, roti and curd fill our stomachs with enough money left for pakora and chai tomorrow. Back to the darkened tracks, down to the government offices and along the high chain link fence to the bush hiding the gap. We push through, avoiding the floodlit pathways to the dark gardens. We find our thicket, the hollows made by our bodies in the dirt accepting our weariness once again. Ashkay lies behind me, I between him and the bush's trunk cocooned, wreathed in darkness. He's always protected me, a big brother I've never had but needed.

"Goodnight sanjay." he breathes, clipping me gently on the head.

I grunt back as I tap my heel into his shin. It's all I can do, grunt, giggle, squeal out, since four years ago, since my family were taken as they burned in that building as I slept. I can't sleep inside walls since.

And I can't tell Ashkay who I am.

I am Sonu.

"Never chose the thin ones. Never go near police and security. And never, never hang around longer than you have to." It was the most Pradesh had ever said to me in one breath, all the tips and training I'd ever got. And now I was totally disregarding him.

We'd done a little bit of trade earlier that morning among the food stalls, a wallet from a back pocket, a money tin briefly unguarded, a bag carelessly placed between legs. Ashkay had it all in his rucksack, waiting near the Metro for the next snatch. No sooner had he left me than I saw him, or they, or it. I wasn't sure, and the throng blocking the streets and pavement wasn't sure, except that it was foreign, very important and here. The army in the city was unusual, yet here were dozens pushing slowly up the street through the crowd, and at the centre … what? At first I thought it was Kali or Vishnu but no, why would they need bodyguards? Bright blue skin, thin, very thin sandy orange hair flowing down to its waist and it walked like it was rubber, a sinuous flowing motion smooth, relaxed. And for all that it was its height that held me, towering twice as high as the people around it, having to bend to miss the power lines running to the buildings, across the street, along the path. A foreigner unlike any I'd seen, with me climbing on autorickshaws and cars to snatch a glimpse, then back down into the forest of people diving ahead through the crowd for another view.

For half an hour I'd done this, slowly working along the street, getting maybe one, maybe two minutes at a time seeing this thing, and now tired I waited in its path, waited for it to come to me. I had no thought of taking anything, even though the bags slapping my face and the watches and rings on arms pushing and shoving called to me. Curiosity plain and simple, fixated on the gangling giant now closing in, head and chest visible above the crush, the shouts and orders from his guards fighting the howl of the streets. Now only one guard stood between me and that figure, looking down at me in the eyes, a lipless mile spreading over its face. And then from the corner of my eye a blur accompanied by screeches and screams, bodies flying in a bow wave as a truck mounted the kerb ploughing forwards. I caught a glimpse of the ashen-faced driver clutching his chest and slumping as it passed me, its wake pushing me down and over as it careened forwards into the guards, into the blue giant and away. The blue figure spun, arms flung at a sickening angle then toppling in slow motion, folding down and forwards until hitting the ground, violet eyes staring unseeing at me, thick purple blood staining the dirt and stones.

For me time briefly stood still, the figure motionless, the purple stain growing towards me, the satchel once hoisted on its arms burst open, a thick silence covering all. I regained my senses into a wall of voices, screams, wailing sirens blanketed in diesel scented panic. I reached out, instinctively grabbing whatever was close as I pulled myself up. Fear gripped me, fear of being here, being seen, of the sirens bringing police, trouble, so I ran blindly trying to put as much distance between me and the mayhem as I could. Past the Metro, past Ashkay until I was breathless and beaten, collapsing down a small alleyway half in the gutter, half in a decrepit doorway. I closed my eyes waiting for the hand on my shoulder. I had been too long in the crowd. There was security. And I had chosen a thin one. I was doomed.

It didn't come. I opened my eyes to normal street noise, darkened doorways and pains in my hands. I slowly opened my fists, the odd assortment within clattering to the ground. None of it looked like anything I knew, each object stubbornly refused to be identified or spark any interest in me. Except one. Small, roundish, grey-green with dents in either side it looked all the world like a tiny boiled egg. At first I held it by the small chain it was linked to, drawn for some reason to it; then taking it in hand I felt the smallest twinge of happiness, even of safety. Dropping it in surprise the feeling left me, returning when I picked it up. I hung the chain around my neck, the egg lying flat and low against my stomach under my shirt. The feeling stayed. I scooped the rest back up into my trousers. All this junk would go back to Pradesh, but for once I was keeping something for myself.

I tossed the junk down in front of Pradesh and plonked down next to Ashkay. I was late and they'd been waiting. Santosh gave me a foul look and Ashkay poked me in the ribs, but secretly they were all glad I was back. Occasionally one would be caught never to return, reigniting memories in all of us of horrors endured in watch houses, orphanages, missionary 'safe places'.

Pradesh had now made his way to the pieces I had taken from the blue giant, turning over a small rectangle of steel-grey metal and orange glass, holding it to his ear then up to the light of the fire. Shaking his head he placed it on the ground with the rest.

"Ashk, where'd sanjay get this?"

"Up at Chandni I think, but I hid when the truck rammed the people."

I grabbed Ashkay's arm and grunted.

"Huh? You got 'em from the truck people?" Indrani wide-eyed asked. "From the ones it hit?"

I grunted. She looked at Pradesh, me, then back to Pradesh.

"That's trouble that is, I heards the truck hit into a vip an some soldiers an killed them all."

"So this is vip stuff is it?"

"Yeah, must be, they said the vip was a, was a …" and Indrani fought for the words for a few seconds "a stalien they said, a stalien." leaning back with a frown.

"Stalien?" Santosh blurted, "What's that?"

"Trouble it is, I told you its — "

"Yeah, but what? What's it's this sta — "

"Hey, shut up! I know what a stalien is, big tall evil guys. You took these from the big guy?" Pradesh looked at me.

I grunted.

"Yeah, the staliens, they live on the other side of the world, the upside-down bit, hangin' on with their clawed feet. When they come here they always fight, drink, they all called bluey. This one called bluey?"

I hesitated a bit, I'd never heard it speak but it was blue. I wagged my head and smiled.

Pradesh grunted. "Ok. Stalien. Probably worth something all this but it's just trouble, too much trouble. Them staliens are evil." He scooped it all up and showed it to me.

"This it? Everything you got?"

I smiled. I was keeping the egg, stalien or no stalien.

"Alright, it's gotta go back, all of it." with which everyone started protesting, speaking at once.

"Hey! Hey! Quiet!" Pradesh gave his hard gaze and everyone stopped. "Look, it's just trouble. It's a stalien. A evil stalien. A vip evil stalien with soldier friends. You know how long it will take till they know who's got this? Then they'll come lookin' for sanjay and then us, with guns." He stuffed it all in in his jeans pockets and stood up.

"I'm not getting caught and I'm not going back to the Brothers! I'm taking this back on the street now," pointing to Indrani "and you're going to show me where it all happened." He turned towards Ashkay and me.

"You better go hide now in case they is looking. And don't mark any more staliens ok?"

I started dozing off in the hollow, trunk in front and Ashkay behind, my hand clamped on the egg. I was feeling good, feeling safe even if I was a little hungry.

Ashkay tapped my shoulder. "Don't worry, no stalien's gonna find us here. Betcha we could take him you and I, don't care how evil or big he is. I'll punch him in the guts and you can jump up and hit him in the balls." I giggled and moved closer into the hollow.

It was the cold that woke me, a breeze where Ashkay should have been. I cracked open one eye, it was all black in front to the pathways further away, lit gently by red and blue lights. I closed my eyes and rolled over, facing Ashkay or at least where he should be. Settling back down I took one more small peep, I could see Ashkay's foot in front of my face, almost touching my nose. I just managed to stop myself from grabbing his ankle and toppling him, something was wrong, his foot couldn't be that big, and the color seemed odd, too light, too … blue? The stalien!

Wide-eyed I could see two blue feet directly in front of me, and more of them further back. Twisting and looking past the trunk, I could make out police and soldiers silhouetted against the red and blue lights. I was trapped and I knew it. No way out, no Ashkay, no escape. I gripped the egg tightly, making sure it was under my shirt. I'd been stupid keeping it but it felt so good, so safe. Not that it was helping much now. The blue feet had now been joined by a blue hand, then a blue face. Its violet eyes looked straight at me through an orange fringe, a small patch of light blue cloth on its forehead with a tiny, faint purple stain to one side. It looked familiar, the one I had seen in the street, I was sure of it. It didn't seem angry, but I couldn't tell looking at the lipless mouth and wide slit like nose, but in any case I'd been found. I pulled myself out of the bush and sat cross-legged in front of it.

It sat down beside me, legs stretched out in front and bent over, but still towering over me, staring off into the distance. Close up I didn't think this stalien too scary, just strange, the strongest sensation being the smell of flowers like rose petals at the temple seeping from it.

"Hello, my name is Rehoam."

I jumped with fright, then giggled nervously. It had spoken in perfect Hindi which had scared me, but the voice was soft and high pitched, like Indrani's. It would have been very funny, a girl's voice from a body that tall, if it hadn't come looking for me.

"Do you have a name?"

It tilted its head to one side, expectantly, the orange fringe swaying slightly. It wasn't hair, I could see that it was fixed to a small band that ran around the back of an otherwise bald head. A strange hat perhaps? I stayed silent, staring.

It broke the short silence between us. "You must be the one who cannot talk."

I grunted, still staring at its strange hat. It moved its hand up and pushed the fringe behind one ear. Strange hands, four fingers like mine but two opposed thumbs, longer, balanced, neat, with one extra knuckle and tiny delicate nails. It moved one finger closer to the back of the ear that now seemed to be half blue flesh, half blue metal. It tapped twice, smiled, then dropped its hand back.

"That's to help me hear you. I can't leave it on all the time, it's too … noisy … with everyone here. So, again, my name's Rehoam, and you are?"

Why did this stalien need to know my name? It'd already found me.

Rehoam's mouth curled up, eyes widening slightly. "Hello. Everyone calls you 'our guy' which I didn't think was your real name. And I'm not from the other side of your planet. Do you live here? Where are your family?"

Looking across the grass and dust, to the lights of the city beyond well yes, I lived here but my home? I had one once, like a family, but no more. I thought of Pradesh, Santosh, all of them and the garbage piles, they were home and family now, all I had. But especially Ashkay, but where was he now?

The smile left Rehoam. "The one you slept with is safe. You have only your friends. Your parents are dead. We have seen many like you here, so many. Do you also take what's not yours to live?"

I always felt guilty, just a bit, every time I'm caught and punished. But how do they know, they've never done this, never had to either beg or take scraps from the road, or do things with men for bread, all of it's worse than stealing. And who cares if a few well fed lose a few rupees? Everyone judges but don't know.

"In my home we take care of orphans, nobody hurts them, they don't have to do these things to live. It's taken a very long time, many many years ago it was like this at my home too."

Rehoam leant forwards, gripping ankles in hand, his head lowered. The orange fringe hid his face, all I could see was the blue back.

"I don't hate you. And I understand. I do not have any family, like you, all I have are my friends and they are not many."

This I didn't understand. All those men with him earlier, and he says not many friends? And he's so much older, older than me, and older people have many friends, big families.

"So you think I am old? Maybe I am, but then again I am not. Think of me as young, maybe twice your age, but also old, older than the temples you visit."

How can anyone be old and young at the same time? It can't be true, it didn't make any sense to me at all.

"You want to know how I can be old and young at the same time?" Still holding his ankles he looked back at me, eyes moist.

"To visit this planet we must travel a long way, very fast. It does strange things to us, it freezes us and we don't grow old while everything else does. When I left my mother, my fathers, my brothers, my sisters, all my friends were there to say goodbye. Now they have all grown old and died a long time ago, but I am barely older."

His eyes now began to drip slowly, large wavering lilac drops that seemed to fall in slow motion. I held out my hand and caught his tears, warm splotches on my palm. My own eyes stung, leaning forward I stretched my arm out and managed to put my hand on his.

'So I understand, at least a little, even if we are different. We are both orphans, our parents gone. Yours were stolen from you, I gave mine away. Which is why I am here now. Earlier today, at the accident, I lost some things. Do you know what happened to them?"

Of course, I took them after he fell, but most now were probably back on the street.

"There is only one thing that matters, the rest can be easily replaced. Did you find a small stone on a chain?"

I dropped my head. He knew I had it, why hadn't he simply taken it back? I reached inside my shirt and pulled the egg out, lying against my chest. Even now I felt the glow of warmth, safety flowing from it.

'Yes, that's it." Rehoam straightened slightly. "You probably get a good feeling from it, but it is special, a thing only for me. Do you want to see what it really is?"

Rehoam reached across gently and holding my hand in his, held the egg between the thumbs of his other hand. As he did so the park dissolved and I found myself standing on a black sand beach, huge golden moon setting slowly over a dark indigo sea, linked arm in arm with a dozen figures like Rehoam. Behind them another circle of fifty embracing, swaying in time to the song made by the wind through the rushes and dunes. His family and friends, mine now, I could feel their minds and hearts, love and acceptance and safety overwhelming … and gone. Rehoam had released the egg, letting it fall back against my chest, warm.

"Perhaps that is enough, a glimpse, a sense. You see them as the last time I saw them, bitter-sweet fondest of memories and one of many. It is not in the stone, but here," tapping his head "that the memories lie. The stone …" and he stumbled for the words "… tunes to happy memories, good thoughts and feelings, the deepest that we have, even buried ones that we don't know, making them clearer, better, alive and real again. Each stone remains tuned forever to the first one it touches, and we can only ever be tuned to one stone in our lives. They are the rarest and most precious gifts we have."

I fondled the egg gently, wondering. One small thing could link him back to his family, so real, so clearly, but only ever him. All I could ever get was the crumbs, the small faint afterglow.

"You found it after it fell from my satchel. So it belongs to you, I can't make you give it back. All I can do is ask you, and if you won't, beg for the chance to hold it one last time."

What choice did I have? I slowly lifted the chain over my head and leaning forwards placed the egg on Rehoam's chest.

Rehoam smiled, this time full and beaming, if still lipless. He was no stalien, no evil clawed foot fighter, just an orphan like me, blue skin or no blue skin. And now at least one of us had a family back – sort of.

"Thank you," the high-pitched voice now quavering but strengthening as he placed the chain around his neck "I will never again let this leave my body."

Rehoam reached into a pouch at his side taking out a small black box. He lowered it carefully into my hands.

"We have bought some gifts for our time here, and I was able to trade to get this for you. I will be the poorest and richest of the crew on my return."

I opened the box slowly and there, nestled inside, sat a black, oval stone. I looked up at Rehoam.

"Yes, a stone, untouched and untuned. For you. Pick it up and hold it until …"

Until what?

"You'll see."

I reached down gingerly and picked it up, cool and smooth in my hand. A tingling and then my hand contracted by itself, clenching the stone in my fist. Warmth, cold, then warmth through my hand. Opening my fist the stone, now opaque grey, sat there.

"It is done, you tuned to it and it to you and only you forever." Rehoam took the chain and placed the stone around my neck. "All you ever have to do" taking my fingers and wrapping them around the stone "is this, and think."

I felt instantly suffocated, my face jammed into coarse cloth, held tight hard against it, unmoving. Panic flashed and faded as other emotions consumed me – love, security, warmth. The cloth now was patterned, reds blues and greens woven with golden thread, the scent of cloves and cinnamon strong, the arms holding me jangling with bracelets. I was six again, I was home again, in my mother's arms.

Rehoam gently pried open my hand, and I opened my eyes. My legs hurt pins and needles, the sun starting to peep over the chain link fencing. I must have held the stone for hours, and Rehoam me. He stood up, offered me his hand. I stood and, after putting the stone under my shirt, took his hand in mine.

"It is time for me to leave," walking towards the small group of people "and your friend is waiting."

I could see Ashkay waving at me, running. I waved back smiling. I looked up at Rehoam, now another friend.

H smiled back. "As you are to me. I will not forget you."

Ashkay stopped in front of Rehoam, holding out his hand adult fashion.

"Hello spaceman. My name is Ashkay."

Rehoam took his hand and gripped it firmly. "Hello Ashkay, my name is Rehoam." He looked at me.

"And this is my friend Sonu."

ABOUT THE AUTHOR

Ishmael A Soledad has read and watched science fiction since before he went to school and thought it was time to give back instead of just taking. Continuing to write short fiction he is currently working on his first novel. He lives in Brisbane, Australia with his long-suffering wife and psychotic cat.

You can connect with him on
Twitter – @Ishmael_Soledad
Wordpress – https://hawkingradiationblog.wordpress.com/
and Gmail – IshmaelASoledad@gmail.com

www.ingramcontent.com/pod-product-compliance
Ingram Content Group UK Ltd.
Pitfield, Milton Keynes, MK11 3LW, UK
UKHW040006200726
13854UKWH00001B/64

9 781976 374371